EMPEROR

GALACTIC KINGS #2

ANNA HACKETT

Emperor

Published by Anna Hackett

Cover by Amalia Chitulescu Digital Art

Edits by Tanya Saari

ISBN (ebook): 978-1-922414-44-1

ISBN (paperback): 978-1-922414-45-8

WHAT READERS ARE SAYING ABOUT ANNA'S ACTION ROMANCE

Heart of Eon - Romantic Book of the Year (Ruby) winner 2020

Cyborg - PRISM Award Winner 2019

Edge of Eon and Mission: Her Protection - Romantic Book of the Year (Ruby) finalists 2019

Unfathomed and Unmapped - Romantic Book of the Year (Ruby) finalists 2018

Unexplored – Romantic Book of the Year (Ruby) Novella Winner 2017

Return to Dark Earth – One of Library Journal's Best E-Original Books for 2015 and two-time SFR Galaxy Awards winner

At Star's End – One of Library Journal's Best E-Original Romances for 2014

The Phoenix Adventures – SFR Galaxy Award Winner for Most Fun New Series and "Why Isn't This a Movie?" Series

Beneath a Trojan Moon – SFR Galaxy Award Winner and RWAus Ella Award Winner

Hell Squad – SFR Galaxy Award for best Post-Apocalypse for Readers who don't like Post-Apocalypse

"Like Indiana Jones meets Star Wars. A treasure hunt with a steamy romance." – SFF Dragon, review of *Among Galactic Ruins*

"Action, danger, aliens, romance – yup, it's another great book from Anna Hackett!" – Book Gannet Reviews, review of *Hell Squad: Marcus*

Sign up for my VIP mailing list and get your *free box set* containing three action-packed romances.

Visit here to get started: www.annahackett.com

CHAPTER ONE

Pain. Heat. Burning.

She squirmed, trying to escape the agony. Her head was a fuzzy cloud of fog. *Where was she? What had happened?*

Who was she?

A shot of panic cut through the pain. She couldn't remember her name. She thrashed on the bed. She hated not knowing.

"Shh. Easy."

It was a voice she didn't recognize. Female, soothing.

But it didn't soothe her.

The agony ripped through her like claws raking her insides. She thrashed again.

"Help her," a deep voice growled.

That voice. She turned her head, seeking the source, but she couldn't see anything. Everything was just a blur of shadows.

She'd heard that growly voice, filled with power, before.

It should scare her, but instead, her pulse raced. She *needed* to hear that voice.

Flames erupted inside her, like her body was trying to turn itself inside out. An anguished cry ripped from her.

"I've given her as much medication as I can, sire. Her transformation is too different. It's gone on too long."

A fierce, masculine growl.

She sobbed through the pain. She just wanted it to end.

Big hands touched her. Heat poured off them.

"Easy, Poppy. You aren't alone."

Poppy. That seemed right. Yes. Her name was Poppy.

His voice was so low and growly. She turned toward the sound of it. A rough hand cupped her face, stroked.

"Hurts," she pushed out.

The fingers paused. "I know, but you're strong. You can make it."

But it hurt so much.

"Her pain levels are through the ceiling," the female voice said. "I don't know how she's even semiconscious."

"Help her, Cassanra," the voice said.

Poppy shifted her hand. She wanted to touch him. She wanted to feel linked to something and not so alone in the midst of all the pain.

"I've given her some aster," the woman said.

The sounds faded. *No*. But the pain didn't dull.

"I... Don't leave me." She didn't want to be alone in the dark.

"I'm right here," he said.

She held onto those words like a lifeline, as the pain-edged darkness swallowed her.

She had no idea how much time passed. When she stirred next, everything had that hushed feel of night. No sound, just a low flickering light.

He'd left her. Her chest clenched.

Then she heard slow, even breathing, and she knew it was him.

Poppy shoved against the sheet, and dragged in a breath. A harsh sound escaped her.

"Hey." That deep rumble.

She finally managed to open eyelids that felt as though they were made of concrete. Her chest was tight, her belly on fire; it felt like poison was burning in her blood.

Her vision was still blurry, but in the low light, she could make out the rugged planes of his face.

A shot of primal fear ran through her. Some deep knowledge in her brain knew he wouldn't hurt her, but that he was a man who was capable of it. He was a man who vibrated with danger and coiled power.

A man who'd killed.

Something pulled her to him. She was adrift, and he was solid.

She reached out and cupped his stubbled jaw. It was strong, stubborn. Even though he wasn't old, his hair was a unique silver-gray color and long. He had it tied back, but there were a few tiny braids at his temples that made her think of Vikings. His blue eyes were a pure, jewel-blue, but when her fingers made contact with his skin, gold rolled over them.

She sucked in a breath. Some deep urge told her to

look away, to drop her gaze. His eyes held pure, raw strength. Thankfully, the urge passed.

"Poppy," he said.

"That's my name?" she asked.

"Yes."

"I...can't remember. Everything hurts."

"We're taking care of you."

She stroked his cheeks—the dips and bold lines of them. She couldn't remember much, but she knew she wasn't normally this bold with men. From memory, men mostly annoyed her.

"So strong," she whispered.

She saw confidence and authority stamped on that masculine face. A man who'd rule with pure strength.

But there were lines around his mouth. She stroked them and wondered what worries had put them there.

His heavy brows drew together. He stared at her face like she was some mystery he couldn't solve.

She stroked across the dark stubble, then touched his lips. He sucked in a breath and Poppy felt something unfurl inside.

But then, in a sudden rush, red-hot pain speared through her.

She arched her back, and her hand dropped.

"Poppy!"

"It *hurts*." She cried out, her body shuddering.

She felt like she was being torn apart.

"Cassanra," her man bellowed. "Get in here. Now!"

Poppy's vision blurred again. The man gripped her hand and she held on to it like an anchor. She couldn't see anymore.

"Hold on, Poppy," he urged.

"I..." It took too much strength to talk. She bit her lip and tasted blood. "Why?"

"Because I said so. You won't die."

She heard running footsteps, curses.

"Step back, sire. Let us tend her."

The fingers tightened on Poppy's.

"No," he growled.

Hands touched Poppy and she felt a warmth on her chest. For a second, the pain intensified, and she screamed.

"I think her transformation is in the final stages," the woman said.

"By the wolves, stop her pain."

"I've given her everything I can."

Poppy sobbed. She wouldn't live through this. She couldn't.

Strong arms closed around her.

"Hold on." Hot breath on her ear. It was an order. "You can get through this."

"I don't want to," she whispered.

"Fight. I'm not letting you go."

Who was this fierce man who fought for her?

No one ever had before. Poppy had always fought her own battles, forged her own path.

But now she was so tired, and she hurt so much.

"*Poppy*."

That deep rumble moved through her.

She heard a dual thump-thump under her ear, and realized that he was holding her against his broad chest. His heartbeat was different, but strong and unyielding.

"Hold on," he said.

"Don't go." Her words were a whisper.

"I won't. I promise."

The burning, clawing pain hit again, and then she felt and saw nothing at all.

"BRODIN."

Emperor Brodin Damar Sarkany opened his eyes. It took him only a second to get his bearings. He was in the infirmary—he recognized the scents of herbs and poultices, and the candles that the healers liked to burn. He'd woken up here numerous times after he'd been injured in a fight or on a hunt.

He was resting in a large armchair, with a small, sleeping woman in his arms.

Poppy Ellison was wrapped in a light blanket, her blonde hair resting against his chest.

She was still unconscious, and far too still.

But he'd take it, over the screaming and thrashing in pain.

He shifted and felt some muscles had gone to sleep. He stretched his legs out to get some feeling back into them.

He shifted Poppy's weight. She barely weighed a thing. She was tiny. He was a big man, and most Damari—male and female—were tall and built strong.

Poppy Ellison of Earth was small and fine. Over the last week, she had been suffering through the Damari transformation, and it had taken its toll. She'd lost some weight, despite the healers feeding her intravenously.

Brodin looked up at his second in command. "Annora."

His First Claw stood nearby, her brow creased. She was tall, lean, with long, black hair—which she usually wore braided, or in a sleek ponytail, like today.

Her steady, near-black eyes assessed him. She never pulled her thoughts, or strikes in training or battle.

"You've been in here for two days." Annora shot an unreadable look at Poppy. "You don't even know this woman, and we have a warlord sent by your father skulking around, abducting our people."

Brodin bit back a snarl, his grip on Poppy tightening. He knew very well the danger they faced. He'd set up extra patrols around the city and the safe zone in the forest. He met Annora's dark gaze. She held it for a second before looking at the floor.

"I promised Rhain and his soon-to-be queen that I would take care of this woman."

A few weeks ago, Mallory West and Dr. Poppy Ellison had tested some experimental space travel technology. Their test had gone wrong. The women's ship had been flung through a wormhole, and into the Sarkany system. They'd crash landed on his brother Rhain's planet, Zhalto.

Rhain had rescued the feisty and dangerous Mal, and fallen in love with her in the process. Despite the circumstances, Brodin felt a spurt of amusement.

Unfortunately, Poppy had ended up in the not-so-tender hands of the warlord Krastin.

Krastin had been sent by their *gorr*-ridden father, Zavir.

Zavir ruled the planet Sarkan. Thanks to strategic marriages, he had a son on each planet in the system. Their third brother, Graylan, ruled the planet Taln. The three brothers didn't worry about the *half* part of their relationship, and were united in their hatred for their evil, power-hungry father.

Zavir wanted his sons by his side. Not out of any sense of love. No, he wanted their abilities.

He was sending warlords from his allies, the Zhylaw. The Zhylaw scientists pushed the limits and would cross any line for a paycheck. They loved to create beasts that ripped and tore, and mindlessly obeyed orders.

Rhain had defeated Krastin, but not before the warlord had experimented on Poppy—infecting her with Damari blood. People on Damar were wolf shapeshifters. Not many survived a forced transformation.

"Brodin," Annora said, an edge to her voice.

His temper spiked, but as he'd learned to do as a stubborn, volatile teen, he wrestled it under control. When he did lose his temper, it was never pretty.

Annora was smart, strong, and often impatient. He respected her and her skills, and she was one of the few people he allowed to push him and question his judgment.

"Is there anything you can't handle?" He arched a brow.

He would never let down his people. They lived with the wild wolf inside. Without strength and a steady hand to rule them, he was aware many Damari would surrender to their animal instincts. To the need to hunt, tear, and kill.

Brodin always reminded them that they weren't just animals, not just predators. Protecting the Damari, even from themselves, was a vow he'd made to his mother.

Annora sighed and sank into the chair across from him. "No. There've been a few sightings of Candela. My team ran them all down." She growled. "There's been no recent sign of the *gorr*-ridden witch."

Candela Salix. Brodin's lip curled. The Zhylaw warlord was ruthless, and known to torture her test subjects.

"Do we have any more missing hunters?" he asked.

His First Claw shook her head. "People are jittery, though."

"Good. It will help keep them safe."

Damar was a forest world, teeming with wildlife. They were part wolf, and hunting in the forest was a biological imperative they couldn't ignore. They needed to shed their civilized skins, and run and hunt and let the animal free in order to keep it in check.

Sometimes they hunted in packs, sometimes alone.

Candela had targeted lone hunters. Several were missing. One, Brodin knew for certain was dead. He'd been used to infect Poppy.

Poppy made a faint sound. Brodin studied the soft curve of her cheek. She was very pale at the moment, although he could see a golden undertone to her skin. She probably tanned in the sun. Her lashes and eyebrows were shades darker than her bright golden hair.

Ever since he'd brought her here to Accalia, the forest

city of the wolves, he'd felt a strange, protective compulsion.

Poppy Ellison unsettled him. At first, he thought it was just because he'd promised Rhain and Mal he'd take care of her.

But over the days, watching her grit as her body fought the transformation, he felt a pull he didn't understand, and didn't want.

He had a planet to protect. People who could be dangerous, if he didn't keep complete control.

And he had a father who would burn it all to make Brodin bend.

He couldn't afford a distraction.

His gaze dropped to Poppy again. He remembered how she'd touched him in her delirium. His jaw tightened. No, Poppy Ellison was a weakness he didn't need.

She'd heal, then she'd go back to Rhain's world of Zhalto.

There was a knock on the door. Tolf, one of his cleavers, strode in. The man was tall, broad, with short hair in a silver-gray color common to some Damari.

"Emperor." The elite Damari fighter nodded. "First Claw." He glanced at Annora. "Another hunter has gone missing."

Annora hissed.

Brodin ground his teeth together. "Who?"

"Fillian. He's young. Barely out of training."

"No one is to be hunting alone," Brodin said.

"He was with a friend at the edge of the safe zone. They were separated for a few minutes."

Long enough for Candela to get her claws on him.

They'd set up the safe zone after it was confirmed Candela was on the planet. It was an area of forest close to the city, patrolled by cleavers and with sensors embedded at the perimeter. It gave Accalia's residents a safe area to indulge their wolves.

Clearly not safe enough. His gut tightened.

"Increase the patrols."

Annora nodded, her gaze hardening. She had a sister just a little younger than Fillian. Then his First Claw's gaze dropped to the human woman in Brodin's arms.

A part of him didn't want to leave Poppy. A muscle ticked in his jaw. He'd promised her that he wouldn't.

But he had a duty to his people. He had to find Fillian. He gently set Poppy back on the bed. She stirred restlessly.

"Shh," he murmured.

She settled, and he stroked her golden hair.

Cassanra, the head healer, entered. She was a few years older than Brodin, with sharp cheekbones, and dark hair pulled up in a bun.

"Watch her," he ordered.

The healer nodded.

With one last glance at Poppy, Brodin followed Annora out of the infirmary.

CHAPTER TWO

Poppy woke up feeling hot. Her skin was on fire, and her mouth was parched.

She turned her head and took in the dim room, and the warm, wooden walls.

Her head was fuzzy. *Where was she?*

Memories of pain and agony filled her.

And memories of *him*.

Her pulse raced. Where was he? He said he wouldn't leave her.

But she was very much alone.

With all the questions echoing in her head, she slid off the bed, feeling the cool wood under her feet. Her legs collapsed and she landed on her butt on the floor.

Ow. She felt so weak.

Think, Poppy. Her head was a big ball of confusion, but she knew she was good at thinking. She hated not knowing things.

She stumbled to her feet, testing her legs. There was a weird feeling inside her. Like a clawing in her gut.

She wore finely woven, loose pants and a shirt, both in a pale blue. She scraped a hand through her shoulder-length hair. It felt lank, and her throat was painfully dry. She scanned the pretty room, searching for clues, but the soothing green walls and the rumpled bed didn't tell her much. There was an empty armchair beside the bed.

A side table held some instruments. Her brow creased. None of them looked familiar, but they appeared to be vaguely medical. She snatched up a small knife that reminded her of a scalpel, and slipped it into her pocket.

Her head throbbed. There was someone she should be looking for...

The pain increased, like a pressure on her brain. Stumbling toward the door, she stepped into a hallway. It was painted in soft greens and there was a framed painting on one wall. A gorgeous landscape of a dense forest, with mountains in the distance.

Nothing looked familiar.

She staggered down the hall, through an empty area filled with chairs, and opened the front door. She stepped outside.

The building was made of wood—it looked like a wood cabin, with an A-frame roof.

Then she turned, and was assaulted by sensory input.

Poppy winced and shielded her eyes. She could barely think. The light of the sun was way too bright, spearing into her eyes. She looked up through her spread fingers and noted the sun had a reddish tint.

Argh. Sounds bombarded her as well. And smells. Below her, a small city lay nestled in the dense trees of a wide valley. Small cabins were dotted here and there, along with larger buildings that dripped with greenery. Platforms and buildings were set up in the highest trees, several with wooden walkways linking them.

In the distance, a green-covered hill had several narrow waterfalls falling from it, and semi-circular platforms built into the side of it. As she watched, a brown ship flew toward one platform. Her breath caught. It had a solid body and two long wings that flapped gently, almost like a bird. As it neared the platform, the wings folded upward and it landed.

She'd never seen a ship like that before.

Where was she?

"Think, Poppy." Her usually quick mind felt like sludge. Everything smelled green—the lush scent of trees, leaves, flowers. For a second, it reminded her of her parents' farm in Kansas.

But this place was nothing like Kansas.

She watched people walking on paths that wound around through the trees. The people moved with a smooth, liquid grace. The smells of people, animals, and cooking cut through her head like a blade. The noise level increased. She whimpered and clamped her hands over her ears.

It was too much. In her ears, she heard a thousand conversations, and someone hammering something.

Tasting bile in her throat, she stumbled down the steps, and noted a few people eyeing her strangely.

Probably because she was barefoot and felt tiny compared to everyone. They were all giants—big, tall, muscular.

She charged on. Her man had been big, too. She

shook her head. She must've imagined him. She felt a sharp pain inside at the thought.

He'd felt real. He'd promised not to leave her.

More sounds made her head throb. She felt a sharp pain in her hands, along her fingers. Like something was trying to break free.

She stumbled off the wide path and into the trees.

Instantly, the sound level lowered, and she released a breath. *Better.*

It was vital she clear her head so she could work out exactly where she was and how she'd gotten here.

The smells were fresher here, crisper and cleaner. She had no idea where she was going. She stumbled down the narrow path that wound its way through the forest. She needed to find...someone, but her brain wasn't clear enough to work out who that was.

She staggered through some bushes. They looked different. Some had round leaves, stacked together like a deck of cards. Others had round, bulbous flowers in a brilliant purple.

An animal darted out in front of her. Poppy barely stifled a shriek of surprise. It stopped, looked at her with huge eyes. It was fluffy, about the size of a cat, and had... six legs. It made a squeaking noise and darted into the bushes.

Poppy swallowed. She'd never seen an animal like it.

Either she wasn't on Earth, or this was one crazy dream.

She kept going. The ache inside her grew until it finally made her stop, and she bent over and vomited.

Another wave of dizziness hit. There was too much input; she was drowning in it.

She swallowed a sob. For a second, she was ten again. Moving up several grades in school because she was too smart. The kids were far older than her, and they'd teased and bullied her.

No one understood her. Her farmer parents had been baffled by her.

Her teachers had been frustrated when she finished her work so fast and sometimes corrected them.

The only person who'd accepted her as she was, had been her younger sister. Laurel, known as Lo to her family and friends, had always championed Poppy. *My super-smart big sister*. Lo had been like sunshine.

But she was gone now. Had died a long time ago, leaving Poppy alone.

She'd developed a thick skin, and a prickly attitude for protection.

The dense trees thinned out, and she stepped out on the edge of a cliff. She gasped.

The scene before her looked like something out of a fairytale.

The ribbon of a wide river wound through the valley down below. The mountains were steep and forested, and in the distance, she saw some strange, man-made structures, rising up by the river. They looked like the sails of a yacht, gleaming white in the sun.

Then she heard noises behind her, voices.

Poppy turned her head, and her chest hitched. She had to keep moving. She had no idea where she was going, but she needed to find... Poppy rubbed her temple. A woman.

The voices got closer. She heard laughter.

"Aamir, I'm going to find you," a young female voice called out.

The woman was close. Adrenaline spiked, then Poppy felt another flash of pain. Suddenly, her fingers were tipped with claws.

She blinked, her throat closing. That wasn't possible.

She heard a body moving through the bush, in her direction.

Hide.

She gripped the tree nearby, and rammed her claws into the bark. Then she climbed.

Poppy was pretty sure she'd never climbed a tree before. As a kid, she'd always been too busy reading or studying to play outside. She hadn't been sporty, either. Even now, the closest she got to a gym was buying yoga pants.

But it was like her body knew what to do. She moved quickly up the trunk of the tree, feeling a strength and speed that she'd never felt before.

She pulled herself into the branches, and went still.

A young woman with dark hair appeared. She looked like she was a teenager. She stepped out of the trees, crouched and sniffed.

"Aamir? We can't go much farther from Accalia or we'll reach the edge of the safe zone. You know the emperor's issued a warning. No one should be out here alone or outside of the safe zone."

A dash of movement, and a large, wolf-like creature leaped out of the bush in front of the woman.

Poppy froze. *Oh, God.* It was huge. The woman would be ripped to shreds.

The wolf was huge, sleek, and more streamlined than the ones she'd seen on Earth. It also had faint strands of glowing blue color through its brown fur, and a longer tail.

It leaped and took the girl to the ground.

Poppy let out a sub-vocal snarl and was about to dive from the branch when she heard the young woman laughing.

Poppy stilled.

The pair wrestled on the leaf litter. The woman stroked the wolf's fur, and then the wolf burst, muscles and bones shifting.

It happened so fast.

A young, handsome, dark-haired man appeared where the wolf had been. The teenagers kissed, neither caring that the young man was naked.

The man nuzzled his girlfriend's neck. "We'd better get back."

"I smelled a foreign scent in the trees. It was Damari, but not."

"What?" The man tugged the young woman's ponytail. "That makes no sense. Come on, shift. I'll race you back."

Poppy blinked.

They were *werewolves.*

Shapeshifters. She rubbed her throbbing head. She was either dreaming, or she'd really lost it.

The woman smiled. "I'll beat you."

"No, you—" The young man's head whipped up.

The woman tensed as well and they both rose.

"I smell something...wrong," the young man said.

Poppy did too. It smelled like harsh chemicals, with an undertone of rot.

The bushes rustled and the hairs on the back of her neck rose. Something was hunting the teenage couple.

"Go," the young man said.

"Aamir..." Fear coated the woman's voice.

"Now."

The woman transformed, her body twisting, melting, and contorting. Seconds later, a sleek gray wolf stood there, with aqua-blue light glinting through its fur. With one final look at the man, the wolf dashed away.

The young man formed claws, long and wicked, and let out a growl. Then he charged into the undergrowth.

Poppy heard the sounds of fighting. The thud of bodies colliding, then she heard the man grunt in pain. She yanked out the scalpel from her pocket and clutched it, her heart hammering. Her head still throbbed, but she had to stay focused.

She had to help the young man.

Suddenly, he burst out of the trees. He looked okay, but dazed. He staggered, like he was drunk, and slammed into the trunk of a tree. She saw a trickle of blood down the side of his face.

A low, feral snarl came from the bushes.

Poppy sucked in a breath. The man didn't seem to hear it. He was too stunned.

She leaped out of the tree, landing between the

bushes and the man. He looked at her, his mouth dropping open.

"Go!" she yelled. "Get out of here."

His brow creased.

Another snarl, and in the thick vegetation, Poppy saw two large green eyes blink on.

Everything in her turned to ice. *What the hell?*

She lifted her knife. "Go. Now."

The young man changed. The brown wolf still looked a little unsteady, but it ran into the trees.

Pulse racing, Poppy faced the thing in the bush. The eyes glowed—hungry and mean. "I won't let you hurt them."

It hissed.

She couldn't see exactly what it was, but she got the sense of bulk, a powerful body. Whatever the hell it was, she wasn't going to let it hurt anyone.

It took a step forward and one large paw came into view. Wicked, curved claws tipped the end of it.

Oh, shit. Her hand trembled.

Then, in the distance, she heard voices.

"Something set off the perimeter sensors."

"I have the scent," another voice yelled. "This way."

The creature in front of her drew back, then it swiveled. She heard the vegetation rustle as it bounded away.

Poppy stayed there, frozen, knife held up.

Moments later, she heard the voices again.

"This way! Something's running for the perimeter."

She sagged. The kids were safe. Another wave of dizziness hit her hard.

She fell, hitting the ground hard. Pain shot through her body, and she moaned, tears welling in her eyes.

Trying to push back to her feet proved to be too difficult. She collapsed, panting.

She wanted her man—her big, gruff, strong, mystery man—to hold her. To make her feel safe.

She considered just curling into a ball. He was just a dream. She was alone.

Somehow, Poppy summoned the strength to push herself up. No one had ever made her feel safe. She had to depend on herself.

She was smart. She knew the best way to find a solution was to gather information. She was good at learning. She had no idea which direction to go, but she stumbled in the direction the young wolves had gone. She tripped a little, trying to keep moving.

But she had no energy left. Only pain.

She dropped to her hands and knees with a sob, then she crawled under the cover of a bush, and curled up.

BRODIN STOMPED INTO HIS HOME, frustrated and angry.

Annora and Tolf were a step behind him.

He'd scoured the forest for any signs of Fillian.

Nothing.

Not a single sign or scent of the young hunter.

Brodin yanked his giant battle axe off his back and tossed it on the wooden table in his large living area with a loud clunk.

Anger boiled in his gut, hot and churning. With a growl, he snatched up a book he'd been reading and threw it at the stone fireplace. It hit with an unsatisfying thud. Spying a small music player, he grabbed that next, and threw it.

The metal exploded on the stone, the innards of the device clattering to the wood floor.

His people were used to his outbursts. Damari as an entire species could be volatile. The wildness inside could be hard to control when emotions were high.

"Did that make you feel better?" Annora asked.

"A little." He wanted to track down his father and strangle him. Zavir was rotten to the core.

Brodin drew in a breath. Right now, Candela needed to be his focus. He would find his father's warlord, and rip her to shreds.

Brodin turned.

Annora spread her hands. "We tracked the scent trail as far as we could..."

"It just stopped." Tolf's voice was rife with frustration.

Brodin had tracked the youngling himself. He and Tolf had the strongest sense of smell among all of the cleavers.

The scent trail had just stopped. Like the young hunter had been plucked into the sky.

"Candela is Zhylaw," Brodin said. "She has a reputation for developing poisons. They say that even her hair is tipped with poison. I suspect she's created something to block scent, and prevent us tracking her."

Tolf growled. "If we don't find Fillian, and the other missing hunters, soon..."

Then they'd be dead.

Brodin's hands curled. "She's hiding somewhere. I want teams up in flyers. Scan the hills. Search in a perimeter around the city. She's not too close, but she's not too far, either."

No, the warlord would be close enough to be able to torment Brodin, but far enough away to avoid detection.

Zavir didn't know his sons at all. He didn't understand them. Threatening their people was the quickest way to push them away, not draw them closer.

Annora nodded. "I'll get Gerrant on it."

The man was one of the best pilots.

The front door of Brodin's home burst open. Cassanra stood in the doorway. The older woman was puffing.

Brodin straightened, his pulse jumping.

Poppy.

"She's gone," Cassanra wheezed.

"What?" Brodin growled.

"Poppy's gone. She was unconscious, and there had been no change. I was in the next room tending Derald's daughter. She fell off a roof and broke her leg."

Derald's daughter was a typical Damari teenager—driven to push boundaries, and with no fear.

"When I returned, Poppy's bed was empty, and the door was open."

Brodin flexed his hand. "She walked out?"

Cassanra nodded. "I checked security. She looked dazed, confused. She wandered toward the main market." The healer shrugged hopelessly. "We tried to track her, but there were too many scents. I've issued alerts, but no one has seen her."

"Any sign that she changed into a wolf?" he asked.

With a shake of her head, Cassanra plucked at her shirt. "No. She definitely has Damari in her now, but due to her different genetic makeup, she hasn't transformed in the usual way. There is no sign of her taking on a wolf form."

She'd still go into the forest. Brodin's gut clenched. She'd be running on instinct and her new Damari blood would drive her to feel the wild around her, whether she took wolf form or not.

If Candela found her...

He burst into movement, grabbed his axe, and headed for the door. "Tolf, get Jarvald and Gwenna." They were the other best trackers among the cleavers. He strapped his axe to his back. "And alert the patrols around the safe zone to keep an eye out for her. Annora, get those flyers in the air. Their main priority is finding Candela, but also to stay alert for Poppy."

His First Claw nodded.

Outside his house, Brodin broke into a jog. He was conscious of Tolf one step behind him.

They took the twists and turns of the path under the willoris trees, whose huge limbs spread out in a wide canopy. As they passed several cabins, young Damari children called out and waved. Brodin made himself wave back.

"Get the others," he told Tolf. "I'll meet you at the market."

With a nod, the cleaver jogged away.

After a quick stop at the infirmary to grab a blanket laden with Poppy's scent, he met Tolf, Jarvald, and Gwenna near the market. Here, more Damari—most dressed in leather pants and soft, loose shirts—went about their business. There was a faint tension in the air, and people were more watchful. Everyone knew Candela was on planet.

Brodin noted several cleavers on patrol, moving through the foot traffic. He turned to Tolf and the others. "I know you're tired from searching for Fillian, but Poppy can't have gone far. She's hurt and weak."

His trackers nodded. Jarvald was middle-aged, grizzled, and kept his head shaved. Gwenna was younger, but no less skilled. Her blonde hair was in a long braid. Both wore the typical leather armor of the cleavers like Brodin and Tolf did. The etched leather had unique designs carved into it, and it was treated with enhancements to make it almost as tough as metal but more flexible. Touches of damar-wolf fur decorated the waist and wrists, in honor of their ancestors.

Brodin's leather had quite a few battle scars, but cleavers wore their armor with pride. Brodin and his cleavers policed the Damari and protected them. Accalia was the capital city, but there were other cities spread across Damar, run by people Brodin trusted. Every now and then, he had to travel to help repel off-planet invaders, or fight rogue groups of Damari who decided to cause trouble and break the laws.

The worst was when he had to hunt down a rabha—a Damari who lost themselves to the wild. Who let the worst of their animal instincts free and hunted other Damari.

One rabha could tear through a town and cause a massacre.

He blew out a breath. Someone turning rabha didn't happen all the time, but more often than he liked. Executing his own people was a task he hated. Damari legend said that the only thing that could bring a rabha back from the brink was a runa.

And they hadn't had a runa born in centuries.

Brodin shook his head and held out the blanket. All three trackers sniffed it.

"Let's go."

They moved toward the market. Along the path, Brodin caught Poppy's scent—light, tantalizing. A touch of Damari, but different.

But it was faint, and overlaid with so many other scents. The others fanned out.

"Can you track her?" he asked Jarvald.

The tracker shook his head.

Gorr. Poppy was his to care for. Brodin hated the thought she might get hurt.

His projecta-band vibrated and he touched it. A blue projection speared up in front of him. He had a message from Annora.

He read it and cursed.

"Some teenagers came back from the safe zone. Said something hunted them, but they didn't get a good look at it. The boy, Aamir, hit his head. He does remember a small, blonde woman jumped in front of him and told him to run."

Brodin fought back a growl. *Poppy*. Stupid, reckless Poppy. Rhain had warned him that women from Earth were tough, courageous, and often difficult to understand.

"The patrols said something set off the sensors," he added, closing the projection.

"Some creature belonging to Candela crept in, hoping to find a new victim," Tolf muttered.

They had to find Poppy.

Brodin crouched and touched the ground.

There. He picked up her scent.

He rose. He had a faint trace and followed it.

They hadn't gone far before the trail turned off the path and into the trees. He cursed.

"I've got it," Jarvald said.

"Me too," Gwenna said.

Tolf nodded.

"Spread out," Brodin ordered. "Find her."

They moved through the trees in the safe zone. This was second nature to him. It was what Damari liked best. His senses expanded and he heard the birds, insects, animals.

Now, he just had to find one small woman from Earth.

"There are fresh scents here," Gwenna called out. "The teenagers."

A sharp whistle from the left.

"Someone was sick here," Tolf said, voice low and gritty.

Brodin's jaw worked. Was Poppy sick? What if she'd been injured?

"I'll follow the main path," he said. "The rest of you, fan out."

His people moved, left and right, until the trees swallowed them.

Brodin went to continue, but hesitated.

He scanned around and scented the teenagers. There was also the fading scent of something else. He wrinkled his nose. Something harsh and wrong.

But he stayed keyed on Poppy's tantalizing scent, and moved toward a tree. He noticed the marks on the trunk. He touched them. Puncture marks from claws. He looked up and spotted a strand of blonde hair caught on the rough bark.

Poppy.

He looked around and dropped to a crouch. Her scent was stronger here, and there were scuff marks in the dirt.

He breathed deeply.

Then he turned and saw a flash of blonde hair. She was tucked into a bush.

Gorr.

He hurried over and eased her out. Her body was lax. Was she breathing?

As he pulled her to his chest, he was amazed again at how small she was. He noted that her chest was rising and falling, and he felt a sharp sense of relief.

"Poppy?" He pulled her onto his lap, and stroked her hair back off her face.

Her eyelashes fluttered open.

"You," she breathed. She lifted a shaky hand and he took it. "You left me."

"Not for long. You were supposed to be sleeping. You shouldn't have wandered off."

"I thought I dreamed you." She stroked his jaw. "I woke up and I was alone, like I always am."

"You're not alone now." He stroked her cheek, and she turned her face into his palm.

"There was something bad here," she whispered.

"I know."

"It ran." She swallowed. "There were teenagers—"

"They're safe."

Relief flooded her face. "Good."

"You shouldn't have come into the forest." And she shouldn't have tried to take on a Zhylaw creation, but that was a discussion for later.

"I…had to get away. I was confused, and everything was too loud, and bright, and overwhelming. It's calmer here."

Realization hit him. "Your new enhanced senses are suffering from sensory overload."

"My senses?" Then she blinked and frowned.

Brodin noted that her gaze looked clearer. She blinked again.

"In the forest," she whispered. "I saw werewolves."

"Shapeshifters. Damari."

"Shapeshifters?" She struggled to sit up. "Where am I?"

"On the planet Damar. My planet."

"Planet?" she breathed. Her gaze locked on him. "Wait." She pressed a hand to her temple, hard. "The test flight. *Mal*. We crashed!"

She was finally remembering. "Yes."

"*Mal*." Poppy gripped his shirt. "Where is my friend Mallory?"

"She's fine. She's been eager to see you once you got better."

Poppy frowned. "Better?"

"Yes. You were infected by a Damari wolf."

She gasped. "I'm...a werewolf?"

"No. Your transformation is unique, less intense. You don't appear to shift."

"Shift? God, I feel like I'm in some terrible movie." She froze and stared at him. "Wait, this is your planet?"

"Yes."

Her fingers tightened on his arm. "Who are you?"

"I'm Emperor Brodin Damar Sarkany."

"Emperor." Her chest hitched. "You turn into a wolf?"

"Yes."

CHAPTER THREE

Poppy walked beside Brodin, conscious of the three big people following behind them. Even the woman was tall like an Amazon.

They all gave off dangerous vibes.

Mostly because they were *alien* shapeshifters.

God. Her brain could barely comprehend it. She sucked in a breath. *Gather the facts, Poppy, and then face them.*

She saw it in Brodin—the animal grace, the way he held himself, like he could explode with power and violence at any moment.

She wondered what his wolf looked like.

She swallowed and pushed her hair back. The memory of forming claws of her own appeared in the forefront of her mind.

Well, her boring life really had turned upside down. A spaceship crash, infected by an alien virus, and now stuck on an alien planet.

A hysterical laugh welled, but she sucked it back

down. Instead, she pulled in some calming breaths. She'd always been pragmatic. She could deal with this. A part of her, the scientist, was actually keen to learn more.

They stepped back into the forest city. It was nestled into the trees, with buildings of wood and glass. Some were carved into the stone cliffs, some dotted high up in the tall trees, and some were more private, nestled out of the way. It all looked blended with nature, rather than dominating it.

"This is our capital, Accalia." Brodin's deep voice held the echo of pride.

"It seems very in tune with nature."

"We're connected to the flora and fauna of Damar. We do our best to live in harmony."

"Earth, my planet, took a while to learn that lesson. We've had to do a lot of regeneration. What do you do for power generation?"

"Wind and solar. In the valley by the river, we have installations to harness them."

Poppy snapped her fingers. "The large structures shaped like sails."

He nodded. She'd sell her soul to have a closer look at them and see how they worked.

They neared a row of futuristic cabins made of wood, stone, and glass.

"When can I see Mal?"

"She's on Zhalto. Until my healers give you a clear pass on your health, you have to stay here for now."

Damn. She really wanted to talk to her friend.

"But we can call her," he added.

Poppy's heart leaped. "Really?"

His smile didn't do much to soften his rugged face, but he sure looked sexy.

Ugh. She turned her attention to the path ahead. She had no business noticing how good-looking Brodin whatever his name was. He was an emperor of an entire planet, for crying out loud. And her life was officially a mess.

Besides, big, gorgeous men didn't pay attention to small, boring women.

They walked up to an amazing wood-and-glass home, with a sharply pitched A-frame roof. It was large, and looked like an expensive version of some lakeside home on Earth.

She realized the path leading to it had led a little uphill. When she turned, she had a lovely view of the valley and city nestled into the trees below.

There were a few taller buildings in the distance that she hadn't noticed before. They looked almost like apartment buildings, but they were wrapped up in greenery. Apart from that, most seemed to be single-level buildings that didn't distract from the view. It really was beautiful.

Brodin dismissed his three, hard-eyed people and let her inside.

"What is this place?" she asked.

"My home."

"What, no palace?"

Rich blue eyes turned her way.

She waved a hand. "You're an emperor, so I expected something big, grand, and dominating."

"Sorry to disappoint."

"Oh, it's not—" Warm, rich wood filled the space. It

had a vibe that said "sit, relax, take some time." Jeez, this place put her boring two-bedroom apartment back in Seattle to shame.

The large open living area was dominated by an enormous stone fireplace that rose all the way up to the high ceiling crisscrossed with wooden beams. Huge, comfortable couches in a tan color faced it. There were shelves of books flanking the fireplace, and a beautiful stone sculpture of a wolf mid-howl rested on the large, rustic wood table.

"Wow. This is gorgeous."

She noted a broken electronic device by the fireplace, and squelched the urge to pick it up. She was keen to see some Damari technology.

"Come." He walked her into an adjoining room.

He was clearly a man used to having his orders obeyed. She rolled her eyes at his broad back. She'd worked her way up through some male-dominated research labs in her time. She never let any man order her around.

As she watched, he pulled a giant, ornate axe off his back and set it on a table. There were more bookshelves.

"You like to read," she said.

"Yes."

She saw the strange, almost rune-like alien text on the covers and felt a punch of disappointment that she couldn't read them.

A thought occurred. "Hey, why can we understand each other? You don't speak English, right?"

"My healers implanted a translation device at the back of your neck."

Unconsciously, she reached up and touched her skin. She didn't feel any scars.

The library flowed into an office. There were more books, and she picked up one. Its texture was smooth, like plastic, and everything was written in that strange, alien language.

There was a huge desk—a slab of red-brown timber. A Brodin-sized desk.

"Sit."

"Do you ever use more than one word when you issue orders?" She dropped into a chair.

He eyed her with a faint smile. "Occasionally."

"And do you sometimes use the words 'please' and 'thank you'?"

His smile deepened. "It's been known to happen."

"Do I amuse you?" She felt annoyed now. She'd had plenty of pompous male scientists shoot smug, superior smiles her way.

"I'm just pleased to see you flexing your claws after being unconscious for a week."

"Oh, well." She tucked her hair behind her ear. "I'm a bit off my game. A starship crash and turning into an alien shapeshifter are enough to throw anyone off kilter."

His smile dissolved. "You've been through a lot."

She sighed. "Yes." And now she was being rude. "Thank you. For looking after me."

He leaned on the desk, his big body far too close to her. "I promised Mal and my brother Rhain." He reached over and touched something on the desk.

A projection speared into the air, the blue light mesmerizing.

Poppy gasped and leaned forward. "Is there a projection generator built into the desk? It must be so small and streamlined."

Brodin looked amused. "Would you like to talk to Mal? Or pick my technology apart?"

Technically, she wanted to do both, but her eyes popped wide. "You can make a planet-to-planet call from here?"

"Yes."

"I need to see the tech. How do you increase the reach?"

"All our planets have relays in orbit."

"All?"

"I have two brothers. Each is the ruler of a planet in the Sarkany System."

"How many planets in the system?"

"There are five. From our sun, there's Andret, which is nothing more than a floating rock. Zhalto is Rhain's planet, where you crash landed."

"Where Mal is."

He nodded. "Then there's my planet, Damar. Then Taln, where our other brother, Graylan, rules. The final planet is Sarkan."

"Okay. How far is this system from Earth?"

Something flickered in his blue eyes. "Talk with Mal."

Poppy felt a shiver down her spine. He was avoiding the question.

He reached out and swiped through the projection.

"Brodin—"

"Talk with Mal." His tone held a ring of command.

She wrinkled her nose. "I'm not a child, and I'm not one of your subordinates, so you can stow the kingly orders."

He growled.

She narrowed her eyes. "Is that supposed to scare me?"

"No, just intimidate you a little." He cocked his head. "You don't scare easily."

Poppy shrugged. "I'm only scared of things I don't know or understand. You appear to love your brothers, and you've helped me survive. I don't think you'll hurt me."

He leaned closer. "There are a lot of people who tremble at the sight of me."

That low, dangerous tone shivered through her. She lifted her chin. "I won't be trembling."

His lips quirked. "We'll see."

The projection flickered and Mallory West's face appeared.

She had strong features, with her brown hair pulled back in a no-nonsense braid. A small scar bisected her left eyebrow, and a beauty spot marked her right cheekbone.

When the brash pilot had joined Nynatech, the technology company where Poppy worked, she'd never expected they'd become good friends. Bold Mal and boring, workaholic Poppy. They were a mismatched pair, for sure, but their friendship worked.

"Oh, God, Mal." Poppy held out her hand, like she could reach out and touch her friend.

"Poppy!" Mal beamed, then bit her lip, her eyes full of emotion.

Mal was usually so tough.

Warmth filled Poppy's chest. She smiled and realized there were tears on her cheeks.

"It is *so* good to see you up and awake, Pop," Mal said.

"Mal, what the hell happened?"

"It's a *really* long story. You sitting down?"

Poppy nodded.

"We crashed on Zhalto. I have no idea what went wrong with the test, but the ship broke up as we entered the planet's atmosphere."

Poppy's stomach clenched into a tight knot. "Oh my God, it's my fault. I must have miscalculated something with the wormhole drive." Her brain whirled, trying to think back to the test. "If I—"

"Poppy, stop it," Mal said. "This *isn't* your fault. You're the smartest person I know. We were testing brand-new technology. I would have been surprised if it all worked perfectly the first time."

Swallowing, Poppy nodded. "What happened next?"

"I came to and there was no sign of you."

That must've been terrifying for Mal. "I don't remember anything."

"The Damar infection can cause short-term memory loss," Brodin said.

"Is that Brodin?" Mal asked.

The big man sat down beside Poppy. "Hello, Mal."

Poppy felt the heat radiating off him. His presence was like a visceral thing. Her fingers twisted together in her lap. She remembered stroking those rough cheeks, and she suddenly had the urge to do it again.

Which was crazy. She didn't stroke anyone. She

mostly found men to be idiots, and was too busy with her work to date. When she did date, it was with other scientists, not muscular, attractive hunks who took her breath away.

"What happened next?" Poppy prompted, forcing her brain away from those thoughts.

Mal launched into her wild adventure. Meeting Rhain, fighting an evil warlord, trying to find Poppy.

"So, Brodin and Rhain's biological father, Zavir, is attacking their planets. And this warlord Krastin took me prisoner?" Poppy hated having no memories.

"Yes. His Zhylaw scientists experiment on people and animals." Disdain coated Mal's voice. "He infected you with the Damari virus. When we found you, you were really sick. Rhain contacted Brodin to help you."

Poppy glanced at the man beside her.

"Your transformation has not been normal," Brodin said. "The healers believe it's because of your different genetic structure. You've changed, but you're not full shapeshifter. There's Damari virus in your blood, but you don't change into a wolf."

She bit her lip. "In the forest, I had...claws."

Brodin cocked his head, something working through his eyes. "You appear to have some elements of the Damari. A semi shift with claws, enhanced senses."

She nodded, twisting her hands together. Of course, she'd be different. Story of her life.

"My healers are unsure where you'll end up. We need to monitor you."

She looked at Mal. "You're safe on Zhalto?"

"Um, yes." Mal lifted her chin. "So, while I was

working with Rhain to find you...we sort of fell in love." A smile broke out on Mal's face.

Poppy blinked. "What?" Mal never kept a man around very long.

"I know, right? Mallory West in love. He's really great, Poppy." Mal's face lit up. "Ah, speak of the devil."

A man appeared behind Mal and rested his hand on her shoulder.

Wow. He was handsome with an edge. His dark hair was a little long, giving him a masculine, sexy appeal.

He ran his fingers down the pilot's neck. "It's a pleasure to meet you, Poppy."

"You, too. Thank you for rescuing us, and helping me."

Rhain nodded.

"So...you guys are together?"

Mal nodded and glanced up at Rhain.

The look on the alien king's face made Poppy's chest hitch. It was clear he adored Poppy's best friend.

Envy twisted inside her. No one had ever looked at her like that. Sure, she had no desire to date, but there wasn't a woman alive who didn't want a gorgeous man to look at her with pure love and adoration. Her chest tightened, feeling like she'd swallowed a rock. Her last boyfriend, Andrew, had unceremoniously dumped her via email. He'd said he was looking for more "excitement."

Poppy sniffed. She was way better off without asshole Andrew.

"I'm happy for you, Mal." And she was. Her friend was a truly good person.

"We're going to get married," Rhain said. "But I know Mal will want you there, so we'll do it when you're ready to travel."

"Married?" Poppy breathed, then shook her head. "Wait, if Rhain is the Overlord of Zhalto, does that mean you'll be...?"

"We're not talking about the *Q* word right now," Mal said quickly.

Rhain let out a low chuckle.

Poppy could hardly believe it.

"Is Poppy safe, Brodin?" Mal asked. "I know Zavir's warlord Candela is causing you trouble."

Candela? Poppy glanced up at Brodin.

"Poppy is under my protection, and we're hunting Candela down." His voice vibrated with a growl.

"So, how far are we from Earth?" Poppy asked. "Can we contact Nynatech?"

Mal's smile disappeared. "Poppy..."

Poppy tensed. She sensed Brodin shift closer. "Tell me."

"We're near Carthago. I met some of the human survivors from Fortuna Station."

Carthago? Shock rocketed through Poppy.

Fortuna Station, a space station orbiting Jupiter, had been attacked by alien slavers over a year ago. Humans had been abducted, and the slavers used a transient wormhole to take them back to the other side of the galaxy.

Her chest constricted. The survivors had made a home on the desert world of Carthago. It was those survivors who'd sent advanced information back that

Poppy and her team had used to create the wormhole drive.

Carthago was too far from Earth to travel back in a single lifetime.

Her stomach cramped. "We're on the other side of the galaxy?"

Mal nodded.

"With no way home?"

"No, Poppy. I'm sorry. Look, I asked Sam on Carthago to get word back to Earth that we're alive. Your parents would have been informed."

There was a rush of sound in Poppy's ears. Mal was talking, saying something about making a home on Zhalto.

"I think Poppy needs some rest, and time to adjust," Brodin said. "We'll call again soon."

Mal looked upset. "Okay. Poppy, I love you."

Poppy swallowed. "I love you, too."

The projection blinked off.

She felt hot, then cold.

Brodin crouched in front of her, and she wanted to curl into that broad chest and let him shelter her.

Instead, she gripped the arms of her chair.

He just stared at her for a moment, then rose. He held out a huge, strong hand. "Come with me."

Where else did she have to go?

But she realized in that moment that she also didn't want to be alone. She put her hand in his.

BRODIN LED POPPY OUTSIDE.

She looked pale, shell-shocked. He couldn't imagine being told he could never return to Damar.

"Are you all right?" he asked.

She pulled in a deep, shaky breath. "No. No, I'm not. I'm on an unknown planet. I can't return home—" her voice hitched "—and I'm infected with an alien virus that's transforming me partly into a wolf shifter." A semi-hysterical laugh broke from her.

"Hey." He pulled her to a stop under a tree with broad leaves and long branches.

Night was falling, and parts of the aconis tree were lighting up. The trees stored the sun's energy during the day and radiated light at night. Damar's moon of Kobold hung overhead.

"You need time. It's going to be okay."

She stared at him, then looked away. "My entire life is in upheaval, Brodin. I have no way back to Earth."

A sudden thought hit him, and he didn't like it. "You have family, or a mate, back on Earth?"

"My parents." She frowned. "Mate? You mean like a husband? Oh, no. I'm married to my work." A forlorn look crossed her face. "Or I was. My work. I can never return to it."

He took her hand again. "Come. You need food. Let me show you some of Accalia."

He led her down the path. The market was lit up with a golden glow and nestled in some rocky cliffs. Buildings were built into the rocks and lights were strung up. The scent of cooking meat floated deliciously on the air.

As she took it all in, he slowly saw some of the tension leak out of her shoulders. She looked around, absorbing everything.

Then she started peppering him with questions. *What was the local stone? How many Damari called the city home? What was that piece of electronic equipment on the wall?*

Fighting a smile, he answered. He'd never met someone so curious.

People stopped to greet him with bowed heads and smiles. Not many could maintain eye contact with him.

He realized that Poppy had no trouble meeting his gaze.

A few people stopped to ask about Candela, their worry obvious. He tried to reassure everyone that everything would be all right.

"That thing in the forest, it belongs to this Candela?" Poppy asked quietly.

A muscle in his jaw flexed. "Yes. She's been abducting our lone hunters. A young hunter went missing today." He glanced at her. "And it would probably have taken the teenagers today if you hadn't intervened."

"I couldn't let that young man or woman get hurt."

"It was foolish."

He saw her bristle. Yes, Poppy Ellison could be prickly when it suited her.

"Foolish, but brave."

"I hate seeing any young people threatened. They have so much potential, their entire lives ahead of them." Sorrow was buried deep in her voice.

"You lost someone?"

She bit her lip. "My younger sister. When I was ten, and she was eight. There was an accident, and I watched her die."

The depth of pain in Poppy's blue eyes staggered him.

"There was nothing I could do, and I had to watch her die."

"Poppy." He curled his hands around her biceps, then tugged her to his chest.

She was stiff for a second before she leaned into him.

He didn't care that they were in the middle of the busy market, people walking around them. His pack was used to seeing him comforting upset people. They often needed his strength, drew on it.

"Why do I feel so comfortable with you?" she murmured.

He lifted her chin, looking into that pretty face. She had a smattering of pale freckles across her nose. Her eyes were a clear blue, paler than his own, that made him think of the fresh waters of a mountain stream.

He knew exactly what she was talking about. He felt drawn to her as well.

But he couldn't let it go any farther. His hands flexed on her, then he stepped back. "Because I'm your protector, until you find your feet."

She swallowed and nodded.

Brodin had to remember his vow. The one he'd made at his mother's grave. That he would dedicate himself to his people.

Turning, he led Poppy deeper into the market.

He stopped at a store that was selling meat on skewers. Several were frying on the grill. "Hello, Derric."

"Emperor." The rotund man smiled. "It's always an honor."

"I'll take three menna skewers, please." He touched his wristband to the payment device. It blinked.

The vendor handed over three skewers of succulent meat and he handed one to Poppy.

"What is it?" she asked.

"Menna. An animal here on Damar. It has very tasty meat. We monitor the herds, and when necessary, hunt them."

She shrugged, then bit into it.

Then she moaned and tore into the skewer like she was starving.

And Brodin went hard.

Swallowing a growl, he tried his own skewer. He'd had control over his sexual urges since he'd passed through his wild teenage years. He indulged his wilder instincts—when he chose.

He finished his skewer and saw Poppy eyeing his second one with undisguised hunger.

That didn't help him get his unruly cock under control.

"Would you like this?"

She nodded.

He handed it over.

"Would you like more?" he asked.

"Yes, please," she said primly.

As she finished devouring the second skewer, Brodin bought five more.

"These are so good." She licked her fingers. "I didn't realize how starved I was."

"You've only had intravenous nutrients for a week, so that's understandable." Brodin made a mental note to tell Cassanra. After transformation, Damari were usually hungry for meat. They'd thought Poppy wouldn't be, but they were wrong.

They wandered on through the market.

She eyed the stalls, nodded at storekeepers, studied the goods on offer. She asked question after question.

She stopped by a stall filled with small mechanica.

"What are these?" she asked.

The small collectibles were common across Damar. Ever since the Damari had started mining and smelting metal, their artisans had been making the small devices. They were all different shapes and sizes. Many were animals—wolves, birds, menna, cats.

The young man manning the stall stepped forward. "Allow me." He lifted one mechanica, a long, female dancer. He wound the side, and the dancer spun. The mechanica dipped and twirled.

"Oh, it's so pretty," she said.

"They are very popular on Damar," Brodin told her. "Our children learn to craft them in art classes, and some adults go on to become artisans. Many mechanica tell the story of the Damari."

"Like this one." The young man pointed to a larger mechanica made of polished bronze metal. It was a sleek wolf.

"That's a damar-wolf," Brodin told her. "They run wild in the forests across the planet."

"They aren't shapeshifters?"

He shook his head. "It's said man and damar-wolf combined to create the Damari." He saw all the questions in her eyes.

"Emperor, you might like this one." The man pointed to another mechanica with a smile.

It was Brodin, standing tall with a frown on his face, swinging his battle axe.

"It's a good likeness," Poppy said, eyes dancing. "That scowl is perfect."

He let out a mock growl.

"For the lady." The stall owner handed the mechanica to Poppy. "A gift."

She hesitated for a second, then accepted. "Thank you." She smiled at him, slipping the mechanica into her pocket.

"Come on," Brodin said.

They passed more mechanica stalls, but the market was packed with stalls selling everything from household goods to weapons.

Some young kids ran through the crowd, laughing. One was clearly the hunter, and the others were trying to escape him. One tiny boy slammed into Poppy.

"Sorry!" There was a contrite look on his face, but a cheeky gleam in his eyes.

"That's fine," Poppy said.

"You need to slow down, Crew."

The boy finally spotted Brodin and froze. He bowed his head. "Sorry, Emperor."

"There are older people and small children in the crowd. You don't want to mow them down."

"Yes, Emperor."

He saw the boy catch Poppy's eye. She winked at him, and Crew smiled at her.

"You...smell wrong," Crew said.

Poppy's eyes went wide. "Bad?"

"No, like Damari, but different."

"Poppy's not from Damar," Brodin told the boy.

"I hope you stay. You're pretty." With a flirtatious grin, he stepped back.

More kids ran by, a couple in wolf form, with long tails waving behind them and different colors glowing in their fur—green, blue, gold, and purple. Crew ran off with them.

"Are you often in wolf form like that?" she asked.

"Usually when we are in the forest, but the young ones are still learning to control their wolf."

She frowned. "You infect your children with the virus?"

"No. Most Damari are born to Damari parents. Infections aren't very common." He paused, not wanting to alarm her or bring back bad memories. "It takes a sustained exchange of blood, so accidental infections are rare."

"Right." She wrapped her arms around herself.

"Let's try this next stall." He wanted her smile back.

Giggles, followed by the *oohs* and *ahhs* of children drifted their way. Poppy slowed, and he followed her gaze.

A group of Damari children sat, watching a shadow show. A man and a woman had a light projector on and were using simple puppets to create shadows on the wall of a building. The kids watched, enraptured, as the story unfolded.

"Come." He took Poppy's arm and pulled her closer.

"At first, Damar was simply a wild planet, filled with damar-wolves, and men and women who lived in caves." The shadow images showed wolves running, and men and woman walking among them. "Then the Radiance came."

The light flashed brightly and all the kids in the audience gasped. They already knew the story, and had probably seen similar shows before, but their little faces were engrossed.

"The Radiance?" Poppy asked.

"A giant solar flare, centuries ago. It affected almost all the planets in the system."

"Many died across the planet, but change was coming. No one knows exactly how it happened," the female storyteller intoned dramatically, "but damar-wolf and man were combined." The shadows moved, showing a wolf and man joined as one.

"We don't have records from so long ago," Brodin said. "It appears the radiation somehow created the first Damari transformation."

"At first," the male storyteller said, "the Damari were wild, uncontrolled. They hunted, killed, and ravaged."

Kids gasped. One small boy burrowed against his mother.

"Some lost complete control of their wolves and hunted their own." The shadow of a huge, wild wolf with giant fangs appeared. "They turned rabha."

More gasps.

Brodin pulled Poppy closer and lowered his head to her ear. "A Damari who surrenders to the wolf, loses the man inside, and turns rogue becomes rabha. They'll slaughter anyone they can, including their own family."

"Only one thing could help them," the woman storyteller said in a low voice.

On the wall, the shadow of a tall, slender woman appeared.

"A runa," the man added.

The female storyteller began to sing a haunting song in the old language. A song about letting your wild heart rest, letting the wolf sleep, and loving your friends, family, and pack. Some of the children joined in.

"The song is beautiful," Poppy breathed. "What's a runa?"

"A wolf whisperer, who could tame the wild beast. There hasn't been a runa born for centuries." As the storytellers finished and bowed, and the kids all clapped for them, Brodin took Poppy's hand. "There's more to see."

The next stall sold sweets. He purchased anata, the berries coated with a sweet, sticky covering. She took them and smiled.

She licked a berry. "This tastes like toffee from Earth." She sank her small, white teeth into the sweet berry. "Delicious."

He couldn't drag his gaze away from her mouth. "You have a sweet tooth."

"I always have. My weakness has always been toffee. It's a very sweet treat on Earth."

He touched a smear of stickiness on her cheek.

She stilled, her gaze flicking up to his.

Holding her gaze, he rubbed the stickiness off her skin, then licked it off his fingers. And he saw something interesting in Poppy Ellison's blue eyes—hunger of a different kind.

He looked away, fighting for some control. She was healing, and alone on an alien planet. He had no business wanting her in his bed.

Looking ahead, he kept walking.

She was vulnerable. She'd been torn away from everything she knew. Changed. He'd promised to take care of her.

Brodin was not in the habit of taking advantage of vulnerable women or breaking his promises.

"Brodin."

He turned his head to see a beautiful woman with red hair and sad eyes stalking toward him.

Fillian's sister.

There was misery on her beautiful face. He knew the pair were close. Tillie was young, only twenty, and finding her feet. She was training to become a cleaver.

Her brother's abduction would have hit her hard.

"Tillie."

She came right to him, and he knew that she needed comfort. He cupped her face and she pressed into him.

He knew she was attracted to him. She was too young, but as emperor, women of all ages offered themselves to him, and Tillie had done it a few times. He'd tried to let her down gently.

"We'll find him," Brodin said.

Tillie nodded, and her eyes closed. Right now, this wasn't sexual. She just needed comfort.

Brodin looked up.

Poppy was staring at him and Tillie. He watched her face shut down. Her gaze dropped to the woman, to where he cupped her face, and Poppy looked away.

He realized that she didn't understand pack dynamics.

"I want to join the hunt," Tillie said, bringing his attention back to her.

"You can't." Feeling wrong and unsettled, Brodin dropped his hand and stepped back. "You're emotionally compromised. You need to support your family, and let me and the cleavers do our job."

Her pretty face twisted, and she stepped closer. "I need... Can I come to you tonight?"

"No." Again, he tried to be gentle. "You're hurting. Be with your family."

The young woman blew out a breath and nodded. Then she turned and strode into the crowd.

When Brodin glanced over, there was no sign of Poppy.

His pulse kicked, and he moved deeper into the market.

There.

She was talking with an older woman who was selling pretty, handwoven blankets. She smiled at the woman.

Brodin felt that smile in his gut, stronger than any sexual promises from Tillie. He headed Poppy's way, but when she turned and saw him, her smile dissolved.

Suddenly, shouts broke out. Two men were arguing at the neighboring stall.

"That price is robbery! I won't let you cheat me."

"It's a fair price."

"No, it's not, you tala-ridden boil!"

Gorr. Hotheads.

The men snarled at each other, and the shorter one shoved the taller man. The man fell back into a stand and items fell to the ground.

With a growl, the tall man charged and slammed his attacker back. The shorter man snarled and formed claws.

Brodin scowled, ready to intervene.

The men scuffled, and one slammed into Poppy. She threw out her arms, shielding the older woman.

"*Stop*." Poppy stepped between the men and held out her hands. "Calm down. You don't want to hurt anyone."

Brodin growled. She was going to get herself hurt.

Strangely, the men stopped, both of them frowning. Brodin felt a strange calm in the air.

The men were frozen, staring at Poppy.

"You can work this out," she said.

"Who are you?" the taller man asked. He looked mesmerized. He reached out to touch her hair.

The other man was staring too, their fight seemingly forgotten.

Brodin had no idea what was going on, but his gut rebelled at the idea of these men touching her.

He moved closer, stepping in front of Poppy. "She's mine and under my protection."

The men straightened.

"Emperor."

"Sire."

The men bowed their heads.

"Clean up this mess," he ordered.

"Yes, Emperor."

Brodin took Poppy's hand. "You, come with me."

"Brodin—"

"No, arguments," he growled.

CHAPTER FOUR

Poppy was almost jogging to keep up with Brodin's long stride.

He pulled her out of the market and away from the crowd. The lights and sounds faded away.

"Can you stop dragging me?" she snapped.

"No."

Darkness had taken hold and a beautiful moon hung in the sky, a shade larger than Earth's. The scents of the forest hit her.

He let her go and spun to face her. He looked angry. She realized they were in a small garden area, with cabins sitting quietly under the trees nearby.

"What did you do back there?" he demanded.

Poppy frowned. "What?"

"When the men were fighting?"

"Look, I just tried to defuse the situation."

He eyed her with a narrowed gaze. He stepped closer, looming over her. "*Never* get between two fighting Damari wolves, especially if claws are out."

"I couldn't let them hurt anyone." She poked her finger in his chest. It felt like poking rock. "And stop looming over me and trying to be intimidating."

Brodin growled.

"Stop that, too," she snapped.

"You have no sense of self preservation."

"I have a brain. I can use it. If you hadn't been...busy with your girlfriend, mate, whatever, you'd have stepped in."

Poppy hated the ugly burn in her belly. That beautiful, tall redhead had been touching him. He'd cupped her face, like he cupped Poppy's before.

It was stupid. He wasn't hers. He'd never be hers.

"Tillie is not my mate. She's pack. Her brother has been abducted, and she was seeking comfort."

Poppy stilled. "Abducted? By this warlord sent by your father?"

She watched his hands curl. "Yes. Fillian is only eighteen."

"I'm sorry." And she was. She'd only been thinking of herself. "Is there anything I can do to help?"

He eyed her for a beat, then shook his head. He stepped closer and gripped her chin.

This close, she smelled the heated, primal scent of him. Her heart fluttered like a trapped bird.

"Do not get between two fighting Damari again. Got it?"

Poppy felt a spurt of anger. Ever since she'd woken, she'd felt confused and like she was standing on shifting ground, but she wasn't weak. She didn't need to be scolded like a child.

"You aren't my Emperor, Brodin."

He leaned closer still, lowering his head. Their lips almost touched.

Heat pooled in Poppy's belly.

"You're Damari now," he said.

"No, I'm not. That boy said I don't smell right."

"You smell good to me."

She sucked in a breath. She wanted to shove her hands into that fascinating silver-white hair and throw caution to the wind.

It was strange, because Poppy usually loved caution.

The sound of a clearing throat cut through the moment.

She turned her head and saw another tall, beautiful Damari woman. This one had black hair, and a lethal air about her.

Brodin stepped back.

"Brodin," the woman said, "some trackers have returned with information on Fillian."

He released a breath. "Call a meeting with the cleavers." He looked at Poppy. "You two haven't officially met. Poppy, my First Claw, Annora Rahl."

The woman nodded. She didn't look particularly thrilled by Poppy's presence.

"First Claw?" Poppy asked.

"My second-in-command. Annora, organize someone to escort Poppy to my cabin."

Annora's face didn't change, but Poppy detected some disapproval. "Yes, sire."

Brodin turned back to Poppy. "Rest. I'll have

someone deliver you fresh clothes and food. Get some sleep. I need to meet with my elite fighters."

She wanted to argue, but now wasn't the time. "You have to find that boy and bring him home to his family."

Brodin's blue stare was piercing. He lowered his voice. "Do you always think of everyone else before yourself?"

Before she could answer, Annora raised a hand. Another statuesque, solidly-built female fighter appeared out of the shadows. This one had brown hair cut in a short, flattering style.

"Jennete will show you to the cabin," Annora said.

With one last glance at Brodin, Poppy followed Jennete.

POPPY LIFTED her face up to the fall of warm water and moaned.

The shower was glorious.

She'd never been one for long showers or baths, but she'd happily live in Brodin's big, rustic-luxury shower. She tipped some masculine-scented gel onto her hand and worked it into her hair.

The bathroom in Brodin's cabin had more wood beams overhead and a huge stone wall in the center of it. On one side was a large tub carved from a gray stone and on the other was an open shower with a stone floor.

Instantly, the image of Brodin in the shower popped into her head. Her belly clenched. It was far too easy to imagine that big body, naked, water running over all those powerful muscles.

Poppy. She closed her eyes and rinsed off her hair. Turning the water off, she grabbed a large sheet that she figured passed for a towel. It was surprisingly absorbent. Wrapping herself in it, she nabbed another one and dried off her hair.

Then she stared at herself in the round mirror above the sink.

She looked so...pale. Poppy had always seen herself as medium. Medium height, medium weight, medium skin, medium blonde hair. She wasn't beautiful, but she wasn't ugly. The only thing about her that wasn't medium was her brain. She ran a hand through her hair and sighed. That was usually the only thing people were interested in.

She definitely wasn't tall, beautiful, and lethal like Damari women.

Nothing about her would tempt a man like Brodin.

Stop thinking about him. Shaking her head, she pulled on the clothes a quiet young woman had delivered to her earlier, along with a plate of delicious meats, cheeses, eggs, and unrecognizable fruits. She'd already devoured most of the food. Her appetite was way larger than usual.

She'd gorged on a delicious, dark meat. She had no idea what animal the meat had come from, but it was probably better that she didn't know.

The supple leather pants fit her well. She ran her hands down her sides. The shirt was a pretty green color and she tucked it in.

Back in the living area, she realized she didn't feel like sleeping. She'd apparently been sleeping for a week. She hoped Brodin and his people were having luck finding that young hunter.

Her gaze fell on the broken device near the fireplace. She picked it up, studying the broken pieces. *Hmm.*

She set it on the table beside where she'd put the mechanica the man had given her in the market.

She stroked Brodin's face, then wound the device. His big axe moved up and down, and she smiled. Pushing back her chair, she went hunting. She found a small kitchen with wooden counters and a deep, stone sink. There was a mug and plate in the sink, but she got the impression the kitchen didn't get used much.

"Emperors don't cook their own meals, Poppy."

She opened cupboards—plates, cutlery, mugs, glasses. She pulled open a drawer and laughed. Apparently junk drawers were universal. In the next drawer, she struck gold. She flipped open the small box and her gaze snagged on the tools inside.

Ooh. She lifted each one. Most looked nothing like what she was used to. She pressed a button on one long, slim device and a flame shot out the end.

Crap. Poppy bobbled it and turned it off.

Then she headed back to the table.

It wasn't long before she was digging around in the broken device. She took her time, learning all the tools, and analyzing the innards of the machine.

"Mmm." She hummed to herself as she worked. She fitted pieces back together.

It felt good. Working was always where she felt the most confident and she could always lose herself in it.

She screwed the back plate in place and set the device down. She touched a button on the front of it.

Music came from it. She gasped. The melody had a rich, powerful beat and she imagined Damari dancing under a moonlit sky.

Smiling, she turned to the mechanica of Brodin. Her gaze narrowed. She pried it open and studied the inside. Hmm, maybe she'd experiment and add a few little enhancements.

She wasn't sure how much time passed, but Brodin still wasn't back. She yawned, tiredness hitting her fast. Setting her tools down, she wandered up the huge, hewn-wood stairs.

"Oh." There was only one bedroom. It was on a loft tucked up near the ceiling.

The back wall behind the bed was made of more of the rough, natural stone. The bed was huge and crafted from wood, with an intricate, carved headboard. The bed was covered in fur blankets.

The huge, A-shaped window across from the bed gave a beautiful view of the forest. It felt like the trees were inside the room. A bedside light glowed beside the bed.

She sank down onto the furs, stroking them. He'd told her to rest, so she assumed he meant here, since there was only one bed. Quickly, she shucked the leather trousers. The shirt would be okay to sleep in. She switched off the bedside light, and thankfully some light filtered up from downstairs. She found it comforting.

She laid down, and instantly smelled Brodin on the sheets.

Breathing deeply, she drew in his scent.

Warmth filled her. God, when had just the scent of someone made her feel...safe? Her parents loved her, as much as they could. She'd just always been too different for them to understand. When the chance to go away to school had come, her mother had fought it. She'd always believed her daughters would marry farmers, have kids, and stay in their small town.

It had been Lo who had stood up for Poppy, and told their parents that Poppy needed to learn. Needed more than she could get on their farm.

Bittersweet sadness tangled up in love filled Poppy. God, she still missed her sister, even after so long.

Breathing Brodin in again, she warned herself not to get used to having him around. He wasn't for her, and one day, she'd leave.

Heart hurting, tiredness finally dragged her into sleep.

BRODIN FACED his cleavers in the main meeting room.

Most were seated at the round table that had a wolf paw inlaid in rich, red wood in the center. Others lounged against the wall.

He could feel the aggression filling the room.

Being away from Poppy made him feel unsettled again. He had a strange, empty feeling in his gut.

Brodin mentally shook it off. He *had* to focus.

"What have we got?" he asked.

"Trackers in the Lantana Hills saw tracks," Gwenna, said.

A projection appeared on the wall. Annora touched it, and a position popped up, marking a spot.

Brodin paced, filled with energy. "What else?"

"They spotted the bodies of dead birds," Annora said. "An entire flock."

The tracker nodded. "By Verna Cavern. They'd been poisoned."

A second spot appeared on the projected map. It was quite a distance away.

Brodin scowled. It could be natural, but his gut said Candela. "Have the flyers found anything?"

Annora shook her head. "Nothing yet, but they're following some leads."

Conversation bloomed, as his people talked, debating possible hideout locations that Candela could be using, and generally growled and snarled.

The cleavers were all strong, aggressive, and filled with the built-in need to protect.

Brodin dropped into a chair and steepled his hands. *Where are you, Candela?*

He wished he had the resources to fight Zavir head-on, but Brodin knew that would be a bloodbath.

Zavir and the Sarkans specialized in weaponry of war, plus, he knew that there were innocents on Sarkan, as well. They were under the thumb of Zavir, and they didn't deserve to die.

If Brodin destroyed Sarkan, he'd be just as bad as the man who had fathered him.

His thoughts turned to Poppy. Was she settled in his cabin? Sleeping without pain or nightmares? He liked the idea of her in his space, in his bed, far too much.

A growl vibrated through his head. He had to get his mind off her.

She'd done something in the market. Those fighting men should've escalated, but instead, they'd calmed down.

The Damari were not known for calming down when their blood was running hot.

He shook his head and forced his attention back to the gathering around him.

"There's nothing more we can do tonight," Brodin said. "Rest. We'll reconvene in the morning, and make a plan."

He let his gaze scan the room, meeting the eyes of all of them. As he did, he felt their tension decrease a notch. As emperor, his strength could affect the entire pack. "We *will* find Fillian. We will bring all our people home."

Nods and murmurs were his pack's reply.

Brodin headed out. He needed to bathe and sleep. He hadn't slept much this week, as he'd spent most of the nights watching over Poppy in the infirmary. He scraped a hand over his face.

Moonlight gleaming off the large, glass windows of his cabin caught his attention. He'd made most of the cabin himself, built from rich, warm, hellobora wood.

There was a light on inside.

Was Poppy still awake, or afraid of the dark?

He made himself keep walking steadily.

He took another step toward his cabin, when a piercing scream split the night.

Poppy!

He broke into a run.

POPPY STRUGGLED WITH THE SHEETS, fighting their impossible grasp.

The pain was back, worse than before.

She'd curled up in the bed. Her ears rang with sounds—the night animals, a thousand conversations, the breeze in the leaves. Her skin felt tight and hot. Her hands ached. She felt as though she were going to burst.

The sound of splintering wood echoed through the cabin.

She screamed again. A huge shadow ran into the room at full speed.

Through the pain, she still instantly recognized Brodin.

He scanned the room and Poppy panted, trying to think through the onslaught of pain and sensation.

"Poppy?" He stooped to turn on the light beside the bed.

She got a good look at him, and sucked in a breath. His claws were out, and they were huge. He seemed physically larger, his chest straining against the shirt that had fit him just fine earlier.

The lines of his face even looked different—stronger, more aggressive.

"I... I can't think or hear. It's too much." She bent over her knees. The pain was going to make her head explode.

The bed depressed as he sat beside her. "Tell me."

"There's too much sound in my ears. So many noises, conversations. I..." She met his gaze. The wild blue of his eyes looked deeper. "I can hear your heartbeats." Her eyes widened. "You have two heartbeats."

He nodded. "Damari have two hearts."

Her eyes widened. "Do I?"

"No. But some of your organs have altered."

"God." She clapped her hands over her ears. "And I can smell you, and other creatures in the bushes outside. Someone's cooking nearby."

"Sensory overload. It happens to our teenagers when they go through puberty. It comes in waves, and it will adjust as your body adapts."

"I think—"

A wave of crippling pain hit. Everything hurt so badly. She arched her back and bit her lip.

"Poppy."

Then she was in his arms.

She curled into him. "It hurts. It hurts so much."

He tipped her head up and studied her face. Then he lifted one of her hands.

"There's no sign that you're changing into a wolf, but you still need the wild." He rose with her in his arms.

She was only wearing the loose shirt and panties, but now wasn't the time to worry about that.

He carried her out of the room, down the stairs, and through the broken front door.

As soon as they stepped into the moonlit-drenched darkness, the pressure in her chest eased a little.

Brodin broke into a run, moving with a speed that made her gasp.

In a blink, they left the city behind, and plunged into the trees.

The forest closed in around them, and the noise decreased a little, letting her think.

He reached a clearing and set her down. He studied her with an intense gaze, then cupped her cheek.

She jerked back. He'd cupped the redhead's cheek, too. The image of that was seared in her brain.

He growled. "I don't like when you pull away from me."

"You..." She swallowed, thinking. "You touch everyone, right? Your pack members. It doesn't mean anything."

She saw some sort of understanding in his eyes. He closed the gap and gripped both her cheeks. "It means caring, friendship...and sometimes it means more."

Poppy's breath hitched.

His strong fingers stroked her cheeks, and she fought the urge not to shudder. The sensation magnified.

"How is the sound now?" he asked.

"A little better." She was so focused on him, she barely noticed.

"You need to focus on turning it down. You can turn it up when needed, but also block it when you need to. Your mind is good at filtering out the information it needs, and blocking the rest."

Poppy closed her eyes and tried. She could do this. Slowly, the sound muted.

"Good. Now open your eyes."

All she could see was that rugged, masculine face.

"Look around, Poppy. See the movement. Note the animals around us."

She did, astounded at the level of detail she could see. She noted faint smudges of color in the leaves—yellow, orange, red.

She gasped. "You can see thermal signatures."

He nodded. "It helps us hunt in the dark."

She swallowed. "I'm not sure hunting small, fluffy creatures is that appealing." The idea of eating an animal, raw, made her shudder.

Brodin's lips quirked. "You'll get over it. The thrill of the hunt is in your blood now."

Her pulse spiked. She saw a smudge of orange in the bushes. The creature was resting on a branch, and was about the size of a large cat.

She turned more fully toward it, and saw it freeze. It sensed predators.

It ran, leaping from branch to branch. It moved so fast.

Her pulse scrambled. Her muscles bunched.

"Go," Brodin said. "You want to. You need to."

Poppy hesitated a beat, then she ran.

She picked up speed, jumping gracefully over a log. She laughed. She felt like she was flying. She felt free.

She followed the trail of color, ignoring others.

She was extremely conscious of Brodin staying one

step behind her, keeping pace ridiculously easily and quietly. For such a big man, he made little sound.

The animal turned, picking up speed. Poppy leaped over a bush, claws sliding free from her hands.

She jumped, and caught the animal.

It wriggled and hissed. It was a ball of white, tangled fluff. She had no plans to eat it. She put it on the ground and let it go.

It rabbited away, disappearing into the underbrush.

"A waste of a good snack," Brodin said.

She winced. "You eat them? Raw?"

"In wolf form." He cocked his head. "You have increased speed, strength, agility, and the senses and claws of a Damari wolf."

"But I don't feel any desire to shift."

"It appears you had a part transformation."

She swallowed. "Can I…?"

"Ask me, Poppy."

"Can I see your wolf?"

Gold rolled over his eyes. He reached up and grabbed the back of his shirt, yanking it over his head.

Her heart stopped. She was distracted by his chest. It was all immense slabs of muscle, with a tattoo on one pec of a howling wolf. He also had a light smattering of silver hair on his chest.

When he reached for his belt, she swiveled. Her pulse pounded in her ears.

She didn't hear anything. The next moment, something brushed against her hip.

Gasping, she looked down.

"*Oh.*"

He was huge. The top of the wolf's head reached her shoulder, and her pulse skipped a beat.

He was gorgeous.

Huge and beautiful, with soft, gray fur. She stroked a hand down his side. Glints of brilliant purple shone in his tail, and throughout his fur.

Gold eyes rimmed in blue looked at her. He nudged her and almost knocked her over. She laughed.

He bumped into her again.

That's when she realized what he wanted. "You want me to run?"

A solemn nod.

Her breath hitched. "Are you going to chase me?"

Brodin lowered his head, his gaze locked on her. She sucked in a breath, excitement whipping through her bloodstream.

Then she turned and ran.

Behind her, she heard the deep, haunting howl of a wolf on the hunt.

CHAPTER FIVE

She ran like a synallis deer—light and quick on her feet, just like the animal.

Poppy was fast. Brodin sensed the Damari in her. He watched her dart to the left, then leap over a fallen tree. Her body was graceful.

He felt the wild thrum through him—hot and powerful. His wolf was close to the surface.

He caught up to her, brushing against her legs. She laughed and he saw the sheen of gold flicker through her blue eyes.

She darted to the right, her laugh echoing through the trees.

He liked hearing it.

She paused in a clearing, her chest heaving. He padded over to her. His wolf liked the way her gaze ran over his body.

She lifted her hand, then paused. He pushed into it.

"Oh." She stroked him. "Your fur is so soft."

Brodin liked her touching him.

"Wow, when I stroke your fur, more of that purple light ripples through it." Her voice was filled with wonder. "I'm guessing it's some sort of bioluminescence. You must have a bioluminescent enzyme in the fur that causes a chemical reaction—"

He nudged her.

She laughed. "Sorry. I tend to get caught up in things. Especially new things. It drives Mal crazy when I 'science speak' her. I'm pretty sure her eyes glaze over." Poppy ran her hand down his side again. "You really are beautiful, wild." She pressed her face against him.

Brodin felt a complex mix of emotions. How could he feel such a strong pull toward this woman from a distant planet?

Then he heard a sound. He nudged her and she went still. Damari still.

They waited.

A mephite nosed out of the bushes.

The animal had large back legs for jumping, light-brown fur, and a small set of horns on its head.

He saw the way Poppy watched it. Like a predator. She was learning to use her new enhanced senses.

Sensing danger, the mephite bounded away.

Brodin nudged her.

Poppy took off fast.

The hunt was on.

They raced through the night-soaked forest. Poppy dodged and leaped, following the mephite's trail.

She was very good for someone with no training. A natural. Surrendering to her instincts.

Then something pinged on Brodin's senses. He slowed.

Ahead, Poppy jumped and caught the mephite.

As it wriggled against her, she laughed with joy.

Brodin scanned the trees. Something or someone was watching them.

He detected no scents or thermal traces. His internal radar told him they were close to the southern boundary of the safe zone.

Poppy looked at him, her face flushed.

It was like a hit to his gut. She was small, pretty, but fierce in her own way.

She let the mephite go.

Brodin looked at the dense vegetation again. He sensed nothing now.

"I've never been this fast," she said. "I wasn't sporty at school." She tucked some of her golden hair behind her ear. "I was smart, and at school with older kids. I had no chance against them at sports." A small, sad smile. "I was also a little clumsy in my teens."

He'd bet she was cute as a youngling. He nudged her and she stroked his fur down his back.

"I bet you've never been clumsy in your life. You have all that animal grace." She grinned. "But now I'm fast."

She spun and raced away.

Brodin watched her, then threw his head back and let out a howl. Then he chased her.

He didn't go full speed. She darted in front of him, and when he reached her, she bounded away with a laugh.

So much life, After seeing her so still, and in so much pain, he was happy to see her like this.

She'd been through such terrible things.

He'd give her a few more minutes before he urged her back toward the city.

"You can't catch me," she taunted, as she pushed through some bushes.

Brodin growled playfully and picked up speed. He leaped into the air and caught her, gently rolling onto the leaf-covered ground.

"*Oh.*" She looked up at him, so pretty with her big, blue eyes, flushed cheeks, and wide smile.

He shifted. His muscles changed and lengthened. A transformation wasn't painful, but it felt uncomfortable as things contorted. In seconds, he was a man again, lying on top of her and keeping her pinned.

Her lips parted. "It's incredible how you do that." Then she blinked. "You're naked."

"Does that bother you?" He was careful not to put too much of his far greater weight on her. Poppy was so much smaller than him.

"Oh, well..." Her flush deepened.

"The Damari are used to changing and taking off our clothes. I left my things back where we started."

"So, you guys are comfortable being naked?"

"Yes."

Brodin's nose twitched as he detected a faint, spicy scent. His gut clenched. His sense of smell was acute, and he picked up Poppy's desire. His cock lengthened, and he shifted his hips, trying to keep it from touching her.

Gorr. Warning bells rung in his head. She was still

recovering, coping with too many new things. He had no right to be touching her in any way.

Then she cupped his cheeks. Ah, *gorr*. His control was slipping.

"As a wolf, your eyes are gold, but your fur is the same silver-gray as your hair." She stroked his stubble.

"Most Damari have gold eyes as wolves." He cleared his throat. "We should—"

She shifted against him, her body brushing against his.

Her eyes went wide.

His hard cock was now pressing into the juncture of her thighs. She could hardly miss that.

"Poppy..." His voice was deep, with a feral edge.

"You want me," she breathed.

He growled. He had no idea why she said that with such surprise. He needed to get up, take her back to the cabin, then go for a cold dunk in the river behind his place.

Her fingers tightened on his cheeks, and then she lifted her head and kissed him.

The touch of her soft lips on his was tentative, almost sweet. He was used to bold, aggressive lovers, but this... this was something different.

His muscles locked. The touch of that small tongue ignited something inside him.

A spark of pure desire.

With a growl, Brodin opened his mouth and kissed her. He plunged his tongue against hers, drawing in the taste of her.

She moaned, her hands sliding into his hair.

Brodin's gut knotted with need. His cock was steel hard. He claimed her mouth, absorbing the sound she made as her body twisted beneath his.

He wanted to claim all of this small woman from Earth.

Then, a faint sound penetrated the lustful haze in his head.

He lifted his head, Poppy's breathing coming in pants. Something else was setting off his senses.

He glanced around the trees and the shadows between them.

"Brodin?" Her voice was husky.

"Someone's watching us." His whisper was near sub-vocal.

But she heard him and swallowed. "A patrol?"

"No." It wasn't one of his people. He pushed to his feet and helped her up. She averted her gaze from his naked body. So cute. "Do you sense anything?"

Her brow creased. "I... Wait." She swiveled, staring at the dense bushes.

There was a noise. A flash of movement.

With a growl, he exploded into action and gave chase. He thundered through the forest. Even as a man, he could move fast.

It wasn't a pack member. There was no scent. No thermal signature.

He was surprised to see Poppy keeping up with him.

They came out at the cliff top. He skidded to a halt. Moonlight gleamed off the small lake down below. They were right at the boundary of the safe zone.

"Brodin, look." She pointed.

There were tracks and marks in the damp soil.

It looked like there had been a struggle. And that's when he smelled it.

Blood.

The tracks led away along the cliff top.

He crouched and sniffed. A low growl sounded in his throat.

"I scent Fillian."

POPPY FOLLOWED Brodin's huge form as he tracked the lost wolf.

She was fighting really hard not to stare at the naked expanse of his back. He had muscles upon muscles, and his skin was so sleek. Her gaze dropped.

She gave a mental groan.

His ass was a thing of pure beauty. Round, firm, hard.

A punch of desire smacked her in the gut.

God, Poppy, a teenager is missing. Get your mind off Brodin's ass.

It was hard to do when it was right in front of her.

Really hard to do when she could still feel that passionate, primal kiss.

Brodin had kissed her. Sure, she'd started it, but it had only taken him a second before he'd taken over.

It had been the best kiss of her life. Nothing tepid or boring about it.

Suddenly, he stopped walking, and she barely avoided running into the back of him.

"Someone managed to disable a perimeter sensor." He pointed to a tree.

Poppy spotted the small, mangled piece of tech that had been gouged out of the trunk.

He crouched. "The scent's stronger here."

She scanned around, testing her new enhanced senses. Then she heard a faint sound to the left. *What was that?* "The tracks?"

"They end here."

She swiveled. She felt a knot in her chest and rubbed it. "I...sense something." She followed the tug and ducked low under a hanging branch.

As she rounded the trunk, she spotted the blood-covered, young man slumped against the trunk.

"Brodin!" she cried.

Together they rushed to Fillian.

They both crouched and Brodin touched the young man's face. His chest was covered in stab wounds.

Brodin growled. "He's alive. Barely."

Poppy's belly did a sickening circle. The poor, young man was so hurt. For a horrifying second, she was a girl again, watching her young sister get crushed by a piece of farm equipment. Lo's blood had soaked the ground.

She blinked. *No.* This wasn't Lo, and Fillian wasn't dead. They *would* help him. "We need to slow the bleeding."

Nodding, Brodin pulled what was left of Fillian's tattered shirt off him, balled it up, and pressed it against his wounds. The young man groaned.

"Stay with us, Fillian. It's Brodin. I'm here."

"E-Emperor," Fillian whispered, his eyes still closed. "Dreaming."

"I'm here. Stay with me." Pure command vibrated through Brodin's voice.

Fillian didn't respond, but it seemed to have an effect. The young man pulled in a shaky breath.

Brodin leaned in and sniffed. "I smell something...wrong."

She smelled it too. A sweet, garlicky scent. Frowning, she checked the young man's hands. His fingernails had a green tinge.

She gasped. "Brodin, I think he's been poisoned."

Brodin's hard jaw flexed. "He needs the healers. We'll—"

Fillian's eyes popped open, and he sucked in a harsh breath. He let out a broken cry.

"Fillian, it's Brodin." His voice throbbed with power and authority.

The young man's gaze moved around, blurry and sightless. He made more terrified sounds.

"Fillian!" Brodin gripped the man's shoulder. "You're safe. I have you."

Poppy shifted closer and took the young man's blood-stained fingers in hers. "Brodin will help you. You're safe."

At the sound of her voice, his noises stopped. He turned his head toward her.

"Keep talking," Brodin murmured.

"Fillian, I'm Poppy. I know how it feels to be hurt and scared. It'll be okay now." The man squeezed her fingers so hard she winced, but she didn't let go. "You're safe now."

She sensed Brodin rising.

"We'll get you home," she said.

"Home," Fillian whispered brokenly.

Suddenly Brodin cursed. "The stab wounds have trillis embedded in them."

"What's that?"

"A local metal mined on Damar. It's toxic to our system, but a necessary component of our power generators. Trillis combined with the poison is keeping him weak and in agony."

"Can you get it out?"

He shook his head. "The healer has to do it. Fillian, we're taking you to—"

"No!" Fillian squeezed Poppy's fingers so hard she felt one break.

Poppy bit her tongue, trying to keep from crying out. She didn't want to traumatize him even further.

"Fillian, I'm going to take you back to Accalia. To your family."

Brodin's deep voice seemed to calm him a little. The air was sawing in and out of his chest. His eyes had a green film over them.

What had the warlord done to him?

"Fillian, let Poppy go now," Brodin said.

"Stay with me," Fillian croaked.

The man squeezed her broken finger and her vision wavered.

"I'll carry him," Brodin said.

She nodded. "I'll stay right beside you, Fillian. I promise. Brodin is going to carry you."

The young man finally released her hand. Wincing, she quickly hid it.

Brodin lifted the injured Damari into his arms.

"Keep up," he told her.

He took off into the trees at a quick jog. Poppy followed and focused on staying close to him.

She realized how much he'd held back when he was running with her earlier. If he could move this fast with Fillian in his arms, he could probably run much faster.

A sharp whistle and two fit Damari raced out of the trees. They had to be a patrol.

"It's Fillian," Brodin said. "He needs the healers. There are broken perimeter sensors—"

One of the men gave a sharp nod. "We'll take care of it, sire."

Brodin and Poppy kept moving quickly through the forest, and then she picked up sounds—conversations, the squeak of equipment, the bark of some creature.

Moments later, they joined a path leading into Accalia.

Brodin didn't slow down until he reached the infirmary building. Poppy hurried ahead and opened the front door.

Inside, a young healer leaped up from her desk.

"Get Cassanra," Brodin barked.

The healer nodded and disappeared.

Brodin strode into a room and set Fillian on the bunk.

"Poppy!" the young man yelled.

"I'm here." She stroked his hair, conscious of Brodin watching her.

Then, Cassanra and her team of healers burst into the room.

When the older woman saw Fillian, her eyes widened and filled with relief.

"Trillis wounds, and some sort of poison," Brodin said.

"Theda, scan him. Norden, get the trillis extraction kit. Someone get the emperor some clothes."

The healers sprang into action and soon they were busy treating Fillian. They scanned him with a handheld device and gave him some sort of medicine. His body went lax. Poppy was so relieved that he felt no more pain.

She shifted to the edge of the room. No one even looked her way.

She slipped out, found a chair in the front waiting room, and let out a breath. She tried not to feel too embarrassed about the fact that she was only wearing a long shirt and panties. The Damari were used to nakedness, so her bare legs wouldn't even get a second glance, but it still felt weird. She gingerly flexed her sore hand. Her ring finger lay at a slightly odd angle, but she thought it was a clean break.

The front door burst open. The young, redheaded woman she'd seen in the market with Brodin flew in, followed by an older couple. The woman had faded-red hair, and the man was built big and had Fillian's eyes. This had to be his family. Other Damari filed in behind them.

"Where is he?" the older redheaded woman demanded. "Where is my son?"

Poppy pointed.

They all disappeared into the treatment room. She heard wailing and sobbing. Then she heard Fillian scream in pain.

"Out," Cassanra demanded. "We need to extract the trillis."

"He's hurting," the beautiful redhead whispered.

"Once it's done, he'll heal."

More agonized screams came from the room, and Poppy ground her teeth together.

His family were all white-faced, his mother's face twisted with agony.

"He's very strong," Poppy said.

Their heads swiveled to look at her.

"I helped find him. He held on the whole way back."

Fillian's mother shifted and dropped down by Poppy, her eyes shining. She grabbed Poppy's hand—thankfully, her uninjured one.

The younger redhead was eyeing Poppy, uncertain.

"The healers and Brodin are with him," Poppy said. "He's going to be fine."

The mother relaxed. "He will be."

Poppy just wanted them all to stay calm and relaxed. Slowly, she felt the tension in them lessen.

As the stress in the room lowered, Poppy felt a heaviness growing in her chest. She managed a smile, wanting them to feel relief.

Then Brodin came out. His broad chest was bare, but someone had found him a pair of loose, black trousers that sat low on his hips. His gaze moved to her, then swept to the family. "The extraction is finished."

"Thank the wolves," Fillian's father muttered.

"You can see him now."

Fillian's mother rushed out of the waiting room. Poppy watched Brodin talk quietly with the rest of the injured man's family. She watched the way they leaned on him, drew on his strength.

When he turned to her, his face looked grim and tired. Did no one see the anger and sorrow boiling in his blue eyes? See the tension in his big body?

She wondered who Brodin turned to when it all felt like too much.

He held out a hand and she took it.

CHAPTER SIX

As they walked back toward Brodin's cabin, Brodin didn't let go of Poppy's hand. She was okay with that. She squeezed his fingers.

The sun was rising, spreading golden light over the valley.

"You must be tired." At least she'd had a few hours of sleep before she'd woken up. Brodin hadn't slept at all.

He grunted.

She felt the tension throbbing off him.

She knew he must be angry at what had been done to Fillian. How would it feel to know that your father was attacking and hurting your people, all as a way to get to you?

At his cabin, she was surprised to see the broken front door was fixed. Clearly someone kept the emperor's home clean and maintained.

He towed her inside, then he let her go and stalked across the living area. He reached the fireplace, his hands curling into fists. The muscles in his back flexed.

Poppy released a breath and walked to him. She hated seeing him suffer in silence like this.

She pressed her palm to his back and felt him tense up even more. "Talk to me."

He made a sound. "I can't."

Her heart contracted. "Someone else then. What you're feeling is tearing you up."

He pressed a palm to the stone of the fireplace, his head bowed. "There's no one. I'm the emperor. I have to be strong. I have to show my people the strength and solid foundation they need. Any sign of weakness from the emperor could destabilize the pack."

"That sounds very lonely. You might be the emperor, but you're still a man, Brodin. You still have feelings." She leaned into him. "It's just us right now. You can lean on me."

Brodin spun, his turbulent blue eyes burning into her. He yanked her close, lifting her off her feet. She barely controlled her squeak of surprise. Then he held her tightly and buried his face in her hair.

Poppy wrapped her arms around him and relaxed against him. Slowly, his breathing evened out, got deeper. She felt some of his muscles relax.

Then he carried her to the couch and dropped down. He kept her pinned close to his side.

"I can't let my people down. I vowed on my mother's grave that I wouldn't."

"You lost your mother?" Poppy asked carefully.

A short nod. "When I was in my early twenties. She died in an accident. I became emperor."

And had gone from young man to ruler of an entire

planet of strong shapeshifters in the blink of an eye. So much responsibility.

"It's hard to lose the people you love," she said.

His gaze focused on her. "Like you lost your sister."

She nodded. "We grew up on a farm. She was outside playing. I was sitting on the front porch, reading a book." A faint smile. "I was always reading." Her smile faded. "A heavy piece of farm equipment fell on Lo. My father was shouting, and I raced over there. Lo was bleeding, in so much pain." Poppy drew in a breath. "Dad's heavy lifter was broken. He'd been waiting on a part. He tried to lift the equipment off her, but it was too heavy. I held her hand, so she wasn't alone." And watched the light fade from her lively sister's eyes. "Lo wanted to be a farmer, like Dad. When I went to university, I studied biology in addition to the subjects that were my passions. I did it for her. Because she never got the chance."

Brodin tugged Poppy closer. God, he made her feel so safe. His hand slid down her arm, and touched her injured hand.

She sucked in a sharp breath.

His brows drew together. "What's wrong?"

"Nothing." She slipped her hand behind her back. "It's fine."

"What's wrong with your hand, Poppy?" He moved fast, using his shapeshifter speed. He grabbed her wrist and she gasped.

They both stared at her broken, swollen finger.

He snarled. "What the *gorr* happened?"

"Well, I—"

"Fillian." Realization dawned on Brodin's face.

"When Fillian held your hand, he broke your finger. You need a healer."

"No. The healers are busy with Fillian. It doesn't hurt too bad now."

"We at least need to move the bone into the right place and bandage it."

"I—"

He shifted the bone. Pain flared and she let out a sharp cry. Nausea swirled.

Brodin shifted closer. "I'm sorry."

She panted, then leaned her face against his chest. "Just give me a second."

He took a cloth from his pocket and wrapped her finger. "You'll heal faster, now that you're Damari. It should be better tomorrow."

She looked up at him. "Thank you."

He stilled, his gaze dropping to her lips. Then he shook himself and looked away. His gaze snagged on the table. "What's this?"

He rose and wandered over to the repaired music player, and the mechanica from the market.

"Oh, I played around a bit." She rose. "I hope you don't mind, but that music player was already broken..."

"I know. I broke it when I threw it at the wall. I was mad."

She tilted her head. "Do you often throw things when you're mad?"

He paused. "Yes."

"Well, it's fixed now."

He touched the button on it and music played. The

deep beat accompanied by beautiful strings filled the room.

His eyes widened. "It didn't sound this good before."

"I made a few enhancements."

He just stared at her.

She shrugged. "I'm good with machines, Brodin. It's my thing."

He turned to the mechanica of him with his giant axe. He wound it. The Brodin figure crouched, then sprung up, chopping his axe sideways.

Brodin shook his head. "No mechanica has ever moved like this." He looked at her. "You're a genius."

Poppy felt heat in her cheeks. "Like I said, I'm good at it, and I enjoy discovering how things work, and making them better."

"I need to introduce you to my science team. They're struggling to increase the efficiency of our solar-power generators."

"I could take a look."

He cupped her cheek. "But not right now."

He looked so tired and she really just wanted to see him switch off for a bit. "How about I make us a warm drink?"

His lips twitched. "Do you know what drinks we have?"

"Nope. But I'm a genius, remember. I'll work it out."

"There's a tin filled with dried cala leaves. Brewed with hot water, they make a soothing drink."

"I'm on it." She left him sitting on the couch and banged around in his kitchen. She found a device to boil water, filled it, and set it humming. After a search of the cupboards, she found a tin filled with what looked like tea leaves.

She found two, large handmade mugs. They were both painted with images of the forest. She poured the tea, then carried the mugs back out.

And found Brodin asleep on the couch.

Her heart squeezed. He didn't look any less deadly or powerful. She set the mugs on the table and walked over to him.

Then following the urge inside her, she sat beside him. His arm shot out and tugged her against him. She looked at his face, but he was still asleep.

She pressed her face to his chest and snuggled in. She felt the stress and worry leak out of her. Right then and there, she didn't worry about the fact she could never return to Earth, or that she was now part-Damari, or that there was an evil warlord lurking around.

She breathed in Brodin's spicy, male scent and closed her eyes.

BRODIN WOKE ON HIS COUCH, a small, warm female in his arms.

He opened his eyes and saw Poppy's blonde head. Her palm was splayed across his chest and he was pleased to see her broken finger was healing.

He stroked a hand down her back and she made a contented sound.

He'd slept well. Better than he'd slept in a long time.

This felt good. He cupped her hip, fighting hard to find some control.

What was it about this woman?

Blue eyes opened and she looked at him. "Hi."

"Hello."

"Well, I guess we fell asleep," she said.

He toyed with her hair. "For a few hours."

Her gaze traced over his face, then dropped to his lips. Brodin's cock lengthened. "You look at my mouth like that and there's only one thing I can do."

Poppy's gaze met his. "What?"

He closed the gap and kissed her.

She moaned, her hand fisted against his chest. Brodin slid a hand into her hair, cupping the back of her neck, making him realize how small and delicate she felt. But he was quickly learning there was nothing delicate about Poppy Ellison. That body was small, but inside, she was quiet, unwavering strength.

Her tongue touched his and he groaned. Then she went wild. She kissed him back enthusiastically, and her fingers dug into him and he felt the prick of claws.

She knocked her teeth against his, then shifted and almost landed on his rock-hard cock. Breaking the kiss, he gripped her hips. "Easy."

She huffed out a breath. "Sorry. I'm not good at this—"

He tightened his grip with one hand, then with the other, gripped her chin. "Whoever told you that was an idiot."

Her nose wrinkled. "An ex."

"Nothing you've told me about men on Earth is improving my view of them."

"I...like being good at things, and I hate when I'm not."

Brodin smiled. "Getting good takes practice." He drew her back down. "Now, stop thinking and just *feel*."

He kissed her again, slow but firm. He nibbled at her lips, his own desire coiling tight. Listening to the sounds she made turned him on. He opened his mouth and drove his tongue deep. She kissed him back, tongues dueling, and her body arching against his.

By the wolves, he felt like he was going to combust. Changing the angle, he deepened the kiss, drawing in every secret of her sweet, little mouth.

With another moan, she rubbed against him, almost frantic. He sucked on her tongue, fighting back a growl at the taste of her.

She made him think of hot, slick bodies rolling on cool grass under moonlight.

Mine. His wolf echoed the word in his head.

Then he heard light, running footsteps coming fast. He ripped his mouth off Poppy's. They were both panting.

She blinked, her cheeks flushed. "Brodin—"

The front door burst open, and Annora stalked inside, her face slick with panic.

"Brodin, a group of teenagers decided to sneak out during the night and search for Fillian. Their parents found their beds empty this morning. They left a note, and they haven't returned."

Cursing, Brodin set Poppy aside and rose.

"Some of the parents tried to track them in the safe zone." She released a breath. "They lost the trail. It was overlaid by a strong chemical scent with a tinge of decay."

Poppy gasped. "The...thing that tried to attack those two teenagers I helped. It smelled exactly like that."

Fear was like a punch to Brodin's chest. The *gorr*-cursed kids. Hotheads, all of them.

Annora's jaw worked, something dark moving in her eyes. "My sister's with them. And Tolf's younger brother, and three others."

Gorr. "Get a team of cleavers. We have to find them. Fast."

With a swift nod, Annora turned and ran out, her ponytail whipping behind her.

Poppy stood. "Candela appears to be targeting your teens."

He ground his teeth together. "Yes. They're mature enough to make good test subjects, but not as hard to contain as an adult." The warlord would pay.

"I'm coming with you."

Brodin frowned. "No, I don't want—"

Her chin lifted. "I'm coming. I'm *not* just sitting here while those kids are in danger."

Her voice wavered. He knew she was thinking about her sister.

"I know all these Damari senses are new to me, but I can help, and I want to learn. I need to learn. Somehow, I felt that Fillian was close. Maybe I can do the same with these teenagers."

Brodin stared at her. At that pretty face, and the

fierce determination on it. These women from Earth were tough to the bone.

"Please, Brodin."

The truth was, he didn't want her out of his sight. He couldn't quite explain it, but the protective need inside him was almost overpowering. He might function better with her beside him.

And she was right. While Brodin had scented Fillian, Poppy had known how to find the young man. How, Brodin couldn't quite explain, but she could help.

He nodded.

"Let me get dressed." She dashed up the stairs, giving him a perfect view of her slim legs.

Brodin pulled his leather armor on, then strapped his battle axe on his back. The few hours sleep he'd managed, with Poppy tucked up against him, had refreshed him. He didn't need a lot of sleep anyway.

Poppy reappeared. "I'm ready."

She wore a long-sleeved black shirt tucked into leather pants, and boots. He closed the distance between them and cupped her cheek. "You stay close and follow orders."

She nodded.

He lowered his head and breathed in her scent. He heard her breath hitch. "Don't get hurt, my sweet anata."

Not long after, Brodin stood with his cleavers at the edge of the forest. The trackers were checking for scents. Poppy stood there, eyeing the trees.

"She shouldn't have come," Annora said. "She's not trained, and won't keep up with us."

Poppy lifted her chin, rolled her eyes, and ignored his First Claw.

"She's coming," he said.

Annora's mouth flattened, but she nodded. She leaned closer to Poppy. "We'll move fast."

Poppy met Annora's gaze. "Don't worry, I'll keep up."

"You did well helping me with Fillian," Brodin said.

Her face softened. "That poor young man. How's he doing?"

Brodin touched her hair. "He'll heal. His family will help him."

Nearby, Annora cleared her throat. "We have a scent trail."

Brodin made himself step back. An edgy looking Tolf stalked closer.

"We need to move," the cleaver growled. "We're wasting time."

Brodin stepped closer. "Tolf—"

Tolf shook his head. "Stein is out there—" With a roar, he spun and slashed his claws against a tree trunk.

Brodin gripped the man's shoulder. "Stein needs your calm, your focus, and your experience. Tame the anger, Tolf. Let's find your brother."

Finally, Tolf's shoulders sagged and he nodded.

"Good." Brodin faced his people. "Let's move, and find those kids."

Before Candela did.

Once again, they were in the forest, moving fast along the trail.

The lead tracker whistled, and they turned into the trees. Moving like this, with his pack, filled Brodin with pride. He glanced back over his shoulder and saw Poppy keeping up, running smoothly.

Fillian had broken her finger and she hadn't said a word. She'd just let him do it to keep him calm and soothe him.

This woman from Earth confused Brodin.

There was another whistle and the group turned, fanning out. Finally, they reached a river—a tributary that joined up with the main river that ran past Accalia.

It took his trackers—two now in wolf form—a few minutes, but they picked up the trail again. They sloshed through the shallow river and kept moving.

They paused in a clearing to have a drink. He handed a bottle to Poppy, and she nodded gratefully and took a sip.

"The scent trail is still strong," the lead tracker said.

"Good." They had to find them.

Brodin eyed Annora. His First Claw loved her younger sister. Nayla had been a surprise baby for her parents and Annora had been older. She loved having a baby sister to protect and spoil.

If they didn't find Nayla in time...

Annora stared resolutely at the trees, her face like stone. His First Claw would be hard to contain if anyone had touched a hair on her sister's head.

Poppy took another drink and handed the bottle back to him. She smiled.

He wanted her.

When she was well, he'd take her to his bed. That should lessen this irrational need for her. His gut churned. Eventually, she'd go back to Zhalto.

She'd make a home on his brother's planet, with her friend.

Brodin's stomach turned over, and he tore his gaze off Poppy with a low growl.

He *had* to focus on finding the young ones. They needed him.

They set off again, Annora running hard at the front of the pack with the trackers. The trees thickened and they moved into an area where the gnalla vines grew. The thick, gnarled vines hung down from the trees, some laden with purple flowers.

Suddenly, they stopped.

One tracker circled, then crouched. He fingered the dirt.

"Jarvald?" Brodin asked.

The man's face twisted with frustration. "The scent stops here."

"What?" Annora barked.

Brodin scanned the woods around them, tension filling his shoulders.

The tracker cursed. "It's like they disappeared."

Like the other hunters who had gone missing.

The warlord had them.

Raw, primal anger swelled. Candela had taken his people, and this time, she'd taken children on the cusp of adulthood.

"No, *no*." Annora rammed her claws into a tree trunk.

"Annora—"

"Brodin, that witch has my sister!" Her dark eyes blazed.

The attack came out of nowhere.

A creature leaped from the tree branch and took Jarvald down.

Brodin tensed, and watched as his man wrestled with the beast.

It was a vaguely humanoid creature, with a lean, muscled body, a faint covering of black hair, and a curved claw on each foot.

The growing anger swelled. Brodin roared and part shifted. His muscles swelled; his body grew. His claws slid out.

He ripped the beast off Jarvald.

The rank hint of decay struck his nose. It was a Zhylaw creation.

Jarvald started shuddering, foam covering his lips. He was having some sort of seizure. Brodin noticed then that the creature's claws were tipped with a green poison.

Brodin roared again and slashed the creature, and it dodged. But Brodin was faster.

He stabbed the animal in its gut, then yanked his claws back.

The creature staggered.

He grabbed it, then ripped its head off and tossed it into the trees.

Silence fell in the clearing.

He turned, chest heaving. Poppy stood by Jarvald, staring wide-eyed at Brodin.

"Luka, carry Jarvald. We need to get him to the healers."

The other man nodded.

"Gwenna and Tolf, search for any sign of the young

ones in the area." He already knew it was futile, but they had to try.

"I'll help," Annora said.

"No." She was too close to this. "Escort Jarvald to the healer."

"Brodin—"

"That's an order."

His First Claw sucked in a breath, then gave him a short nod. She swiveled, stalked over to Jarvald and Luka, then the trio disappeared into the trees.

Gwenna and Tolf returned a moment later. The harsh set of Tolf's face was all the answer Brodin needed.

"Nothing, sire," Gwenna said.

Gorr. "Everyone, back to Accalia. We'll make a plan on how to find them."

Brodin stayed at the back of the pack, anger boiling, his senses alert.

If Candela hurt any of those young ones...

His claws pricked his skin. He hadn't protected them, but he'd get them home.

"Brodin?"

Poppy's quiet voice. They'd reached the outskirts of Accalia, and he watched his people head into the city.

"I'm sorry about the kids."

It didn't matter. He'd use all his strength and skills to find them. He was the emperor because of his strength and power.

Poppy touched his arm.

"Try not to worry. I know it's easier said than done, believe me." She stroked his arm. "But we have to believe that they'll be okay."

Warmth spread through him. He felt his muscles ease, the worry dull, and his anger start to settle.

He frowned.

Without warning, his claws retracted. He wanted to pull her close and just hold her.

Instead, he stumbled back. "What in *gorr*'s name are you doing to me?"

Her blue eyes went wide. "Nothing. I just wanted to help—"

"By neutering me?"

She flinched.

"Something you're doing is calming my wolf. It's dulling my senses, my edge. The strength I need to protect my people."

"Brodin—"

"Don't do it again." His anger was back now, in full force and molten hot. "Stay away from me."

She looked like he'd slapped her in the face.

Shoving his guilt away, he strode off.

POPPY SAT on the tree branch, her chin on her knees.

The afternoon sun was spreading an orange glow over the forest city.

It didn't make her feel better. Inside, she felt cold.

She sniffed. She hadn't meant to make Brodin angry. She'd seen his pain, and wanted to make him feel better. They'd connected earlier in his cabin, and she'd just thought...

Ugh. She'd just made it worse.

She rubbed her cheek on her knee.

She had strange new abilities and powers, but his harsh words reminded her that despite her Damari transformation, she wasn't really Damari. She didn't know what the hell she was.

She couldn't shift into a wolf. She was just a pale imitation.

Once again, she was out of step with the people around her.

You're weird, Ellison. Too young, not normal, too odd, too boring.

She closed her eyes for a second. She wondered what it felt like to belong somewhere. Maybe she would on Zhalto.

Mal wanted Poppy to go there. To make a home there. Poppy would talk to the healers about leaving as soon as she could.

A weird tug pulled in her belly. A part of her didn't want to go.

A part of her felt the call of the forest around her.

But Brodin didn't want her here, and she'd already taken up too much of his time. He had a dangerous situation to deal with, and it was clear she was just in the way.

She blew out a shaky breath. She wondered how poor Fillian was.

She lifted her head and watched the sun lower toward the horizon. The forest looked bathed in light.

So beautiful.

Something about it really called to her.

The same way Brodin did. Her stomach cramped.

She let out a low growl. She *had* to stop thinking about him.

He is not for you, Poppy Ellison.

His focus was on the missing kids, and beating Candela. Her chest tightened. God, she hoped the teenagers were okay.

This warlord Candela was pure evil, taking and hurting kids. Clearly, the Zhylaw and Zavir would cross any boundary.

She heard footsteps and saw Annora's tall, lean form appear. The woman's head was bent, her body as tense as a bow. She paced under the trees, her hands on the back of her neck.

She was visibly upset.

Something told Poppy that Annora didn't show her emotions very easily.

Poppy warred with herself. She was the last person Annora would want to talk to. As Brodin had made clear, she was an outsider. Trying to help was not appreciated.

Except Poppy didn't have it in her to just sit there while Annora was upset.

Dammit. She pushed off the branch and landed on her feet—graceful and coordinated. Wow, that was going to take some getting used to.

Annora's head whipped up, her dark ponytail bobbing behind her. Her gaze was like a black laser beam.

Poppy squared her shoulders. "Are you all right?"

"Fine." The word was clipped, terse.

Well, then. "Great." Poppy swiveled and started to walk away.

"My little sister is missing. Candela has her." There was a growl in Annora's voice. "I can't stand it!"

Poppy turned.

Annora's hand snapped out and she grabbed Poppy's arm. "If that *gorr*-rotten witch hurts her, or—" The First Claw's voice cracked.

Sympathy hit Poppy. She squeezed Annora's hand. "Be strong. Search for her and *never* give up. After our crash, I don't remember much, but the warlord Krastin had me." She shuddered. "My friend Mal *never* gave up looking for me. She kept searching until she freed me."

Annora nodded, her jaw tight.

"What's your sister's name?" Poppy asked.

"Nayla."

"Is she like you? A warrior?"

"No." Annora smiled, her expression softening. "She's sweet, kind, smart. Everyone likes her." The woman cocked her head. "Actually, you remind me of her a bit."

Poppy blinked.

"Nayla's tough inside. Quietly confident."

Poppy nodded. "Then she'll be waiting for you. She'll be smart, and be waiting for you to rescue her."

That feeling of heaviness grew in Poppy's chest again, but as she watched, Annora seemed to relax and was less tense.

The woman's dark eyes were on Poppy. "I will confess that I didn't like you at first. Brodin seems... entranced by you. I'm here to protect him from anything that might hurt him."

"I'd never hurt him." Poppy's gut knotted. "He's just helping me. A promise to his brother and my friend."

"It's more than that, and you know it."

Poppy lifted her chin. "Well, I think he feels I'm making him...weak. He told me to stay away."

Annora looked up at the trees. "Idiot."

"I'm going to talk to the healers and get approval to leave for Zhalto."

Annora's dark gaze narrowed. "I haven't let myself get to know you. I'm sorry for that." The First Claw wrinkled her nose. "I'm known for quick decisions, and it also makes me quick to judge."

"It's fine, Annora. I won't be here long." Poppy's throat tightened. "I haven't transformed into a full Damari. I'll be leaving soon. I can't get back to my planet—" she felt a shot of sadness "—but my best friend Mal is on Zhalto."

Annora studied her for a long moment, and Poppy got the feeling that Brodin's First Claw didn't miss anything.

"Thank you for coming to talk to me. I'm well aware you didn't have to."

"I didn't do it for you. I did it to know that I did the right thing." Poppy squeezed Annora's hand again. "Your sister needs your strength. She needs your quick decisions. Don't give up."

Emotion flowed over the tough woman's face. Suddenly, she pulled Poppy in for a hard hug.

Surprised, Poppy hugged her back, and the contact made her realize how much she missed Mal.

She hugged Annora tighter, and felt the woman relax

more, while the pressure inside Poppy's chest grew denser.

She frowned. Something was happening to her.

Annora stepped back and smiled. "Thank you, Poppy. I actually feel so much better."

Poppy nodded.

"And...Brodin often loses his temper and says things he regrets."

Poppy looked at her shoes. "Sure."

"I'll see you later." Annora strode off, her long legs eating up the ground. She looked energized, less burdened.

Poppy pressed a hand to her chest—meanwhile, she felt tight and heavy. A bad taste filled her mouth.

She headed back to Brodin's cabin, feeling worse with each step. Her stomach felt as though it had a rock in it, and she felt a confusing mess of sad, mad, and scared.

Her vision wavered.

The cabin came into view. Gritting her teeth, she kept going, but the last few meters felt endless.

It took her three tries to get the door open. She staggered inside and knocked over a chair. The pressure inside her hurt so much.

Another step, then she collapsed.

CHAPTER SEVEN

Brodin finished meeting with his trackers and stomped out of the lodge. It was late afternoon, and exhaustion was tugging at him.

He was pissed off at himself.

He'd been a *gorr* to Poppy.

He scraped a hand through his hair. He'd been angry and feeling guilty, and tired. She'd tried to help, and he'd taken it out on her.

He needed to find her and apologize.

"Gorr," he muttered.

Worry for the kids was eating at him as well.

Jennete walked past and Brodin held up a hand. "Have you seen Annora?"

"In the dining hall."

Brodin changed direction and headed that way. He wanted to take his First Claw's pulse. He didn't want to lock her down, but worry for her sister would test her control.

After that, he'd find Poppy.

He walked into the dining hall. His trackers were seated at the table, huddled over plates filled with cooked meats and eggs. Baskets of berries sat in the center of the table—all rich in nutrients. There were also several steaming mugs of cinnamae.

He scanned the room and saw Annora carrying a plate from the kitchen. He changed directions to intercept her.

She spied him and nodded.

She looked...okay. The lines of tension around her mouth weren't as deep as they had been.

"Any news?" Annora asked.

"Nothing yet. We have more flyers in the air, and the trackers are following every lead."

Her shoulders sagged.

He gripped her arm. "We're going to find them. How are your parents?"

"Holding up. Just."

"And you?"

"I'm holding it together, as well." She blew out a breath. "I was murderous earlier, but I ran into Poppy."

Brodin stiffened.

"We talked, and she made me feel calmer. She's been through a *gorr*-ridden situation and survived. I can't give up hope."

Poppy had been through so much, and then he'd yelled at her.

He saw Annora eyeing him.

"I think she can calm wolves," he said.

Annora's brows creased. "You mean like a healer?"

"Maybe." Some healers had the ability to radiate calm, but nothing like the effect Poppy had. No healer had ever calmed Brodin down, or been able to stop fighting Damari. "I need to talk with Cassanra."

"If Poppy can, I don't think she knows about it."

He rubbed the back of his neck. "Yes. Do you know where she is?"

Annora shook her head. "It's been about an hour since I saw her. She might be with the healers."

He tensed. "Healers? Why?" Was she injured?

"She wants permission to leave. To go to Zhalto."

Brodin felt as though he'd taken claws to the stomach. "She can't leave," he growled. "I forbid it."

"Really?" Annora cocked her head. "Poppy said you told her to stay away. She said that she's not really Damari, and doesn't belong here. Doesn't that mean you want her to go?"

He felt his claws pressing against skin. He clenched his jaw.

"You hurt her, Brodin."

"I know. I'll fix it." He studied his First Claw. "I thought you didn't like her?"

"I didn't let myself get to know her. I saw her as an outsider, monopolizing your time. Then she helped in the forest, and I talked with her. I like her. Fix it, Brodin."

He nodded, then swiveled and strode out. He followed the paths of the city, but didn't see Poppy. He also didn't pick up any trace of her scent.

He headed back to his cabin, mentally cursing himself. When he got closer, he scented her.

"Poppy?" He stepped inside.

Her scent was stronger.

He moved from the entry to the living area, and noticed a chair was tipped over. His pulse spiked. Then, his gaze landed on slim legs extending from behind the couch.

Heart racing, he rushed toward her.

"Poppy!"

She was lying on her belly, one arm outstretched.

"*Poppy.*" He pressed a finger to her neck and felt her pulse. Relief thundered through him.

Gently, he rolled her on her side. He couldn't see any injuries.

She groaned, curling in on herself.

"Poppy, what's wrong?"

"Hurts." Her eyes opened. The blue was filled with streaks of black.

What in gorr*'s name?*

He stroked her hair back. "Where does it hurt?"

"Stomach. Chest." She groaned again.

He scooped her up. He kept her tight against his chest as he sprinted toward the infirmary.

When he rushed through the doors, he bellowed, "Cassanra!"

The healer appeared, saw the unconscious Poppy, and waved him into a treatment room.

He laid her on the bunk and Cassanra checked her over. The healer frowned, and pulled out a scanner.

"Norden, make up some willoa. It will help ease her pain."

"What's wrong with her?" Brodin demanded.

"I don't know, yet." Cassanra studied the scan. "She has both an elevated pulse and respiration."

"She said her stomach and chest hurt. And look at her eyes."

The healer did, her frown deepening. "We'll take care of her, sire. Step back, now."

Brodin paced, staring at Poppy, willing her to get better.

Finally, the medicines worked to ease her pain, and her tense body relaxed. Moments later, her eyes opened. He was relieved to see that they were back to her normal blue.

"What happened?" She groggily sat up.

"You tell us," Cassanra said, gently, a hand on Poppy's back.

Poppy spotted Brodin and looked away.

No. His wolf didn't like that. At all. He stomped forward and took her hand.

She tried to pull it away, but he held on tight.

"I saw Annora," Poppy said. "She was really worried about her sister and the teenagers. Then I felt this heaviness in my chest." She pressed a fist against it. "I felt it earlier too. When we brought Fillian in. I was in pain, and I collapsed in Brodin's cabin. It really hurt."

The healer frowned.

"I spoke with Annora," Brodin said. "She said that Poppy calmed her."

Poppy stiffened. "I didn't do anything."

"She calmed my rage, as well. And two fighting men in the market."

The healer gasped. "Are you sure?"

"I didn't do a single thing except be nice." Poppy tugged her hand free and glared at Brodin.

"I'm sorry, Poppy. I was angry and I was a *gorr* to you." He cupped her cheek. "I said things I didn't mean."

She looked resolutely at Cassanra. "I wanted to ask if I can go to Zhalto."

Brodin growled. All the healers in the room froze. "No."

Poppy glared at him. "I wasn't asking you."

"In light of your collapse," Cassanra said, lightly, "I don't think that's wise."

Poppy's shoulders drooped.

"I want to run more tests, but..." The healer's voice faded away and she frowned, staring at Poppy.

Brodin scowled, the hackles on his neck rising. "What?"

"There hasn't been one for centuries," Cassanra said, softly. "Everyone believed that they'd died out."

"Are you telling me what I think you are?" Brodin asked, certain he already knew the answer.

"I think Poppy is a runa."

He stilled, the confirmation of his vague suspicion still a shock. "A wolf whisperer?"

Cassanra nodded.

"A runa?" Poppy said. "Like from the shadow show. The one who stopped the warring packs and rogues."

"A special Damari who can soothe a wild wolf, calm them," he said. "Many once lived among us. They were revered, and held places of honor among us."

"But, why were they so special?" Poppy asked.

"They lowered the volatility and in-fighting," Brodin said. "Since we lost them, we have to rely on strict control."

Something flashed on her face. "And on the unwavering strength of the emperor to hold everyone in check."

He nodded.

"They also lowered the rates of Damari turning rabha," Cassanra said. "It was almost unheard of in the old records. Now, we have several cases a year." She flicked a glance at Brodin.

And it fell to him to hunt and execute them.

"Like I said, I would like to run more tests, and go through the archives on runas. She needs rest and food for now. I'll arrange—"

"I'll take care of her." He lifted Poppy into his arms.

Cassanra huffed. "She needs to be monitored—"

"I'll do it."

"I can stay here," Poppy said, weakly struggling in his arms.

"You're coming to my place."

POPPY STAYED silent as Brodin carried her into his huge, beautiful cabin.

Trying to ignore him, she eyed the huge fireplace. She wondered what it looked like when flames were crackling within. She'd add some greenery to the place, some plants or flowers, and some red accent cushions on the couch.

Stop decorating the man's house.

He was bossy and overbearing. And she'd be leaving soon.

He strode up the stairs to the bedroom.

He set her on the bed.

"Get comfortable. I'll bring you some food."

He was gone, moving in that silent way of his. She settled against the mound of pillows, trying not to breath in Brodin's scent.

The pain was gone, and she felt better now.

Was she a runa? She rubbed her temple. What did that even mean?

She wouldn't be staying that long, but damn, the scientist in her wanted to know. Curiosity welled.

Soon, Brodin was back, carrying a tray, and delicious smells wafted her way.

"Osage broth, and some freshly baked caltha. There's also a bowl of anata. The berries are good for you." He set it down beside the bed.

Suddenly, she was starving. She scooted over and picked up the spoon.

"It smells so good." She tried the soup and barely stifled a moan.

He looked very satisfied as she ate.

"Do you miss your planet?" he asked, after a few moments.

"Yes." She swallowed a mouthful of the bread-like caltha. "I mean, a part of me is terrified knowing that there's no way home." A lump formed in her throat. "My employer, Nynatech, will no doubt keep testing the wormhole drive technology." She shrugged a shoulder. "But realistically, it'll be decades before they can perfect it. If ever."

"Your family?" He touched her hand.

God, she could feel the heat pumping off his skin.

"Just my parents." A sad smile crossed her face. "They'll be sad, but I left home a long time ago. I went to high school and university early, and never went back to the farm. My poor parents are lovely, small-town folk. They didn't understand a young daughter who craved stimulation, and loved quadratic equations and string theory."

"You didn't fit."

She gave a small laugh. "I've never fit anywhere. Enough about me." She hesitated. "You said your mother died."

He stilled, and his face shut down.

Poppy froze. "Sorry, forget I said anything—"

"My mother and stepfather died suddenly, several years ago. It was an accident in the forest. A landslide caught them."

"Brodin, I'm sorry." Poppy touched him, then snatched her hand away.

He caught her fingers and pulled her hand back.

"What if I accidentally do my voodoo on you?"

He cocked a brow. "Voodoo?"

"Weird magic."

"It's okay, Poppy."

Slowly, her fingers unfurled, and she pressed her palm to his bicep.

"So, your biological father..."

Brodin gave a harsh laugh. "King Zavir Sarkany. The most power-hungry, tyrannical man in five systems." Brodin exhaled softly. "The Sarkany System has five planets orbiting a red giant sun. You already know that the Radiance cut through the system centuries ago. The closest planet, Andret, was decimated. The atmosphere was ripped away during the flare, and the people killed."

"That's horrible."

"Rhain's planet, Zhalto, had a strong magnetic field. It offered them some protection, but the Zhaltons were irradiated. The people were changed, and they adapted to use the charged energy particles in the magnetic field. They can charge weapons and equipment, generate energy pulses."

She gasped. "That's incredible. I'd love to study their biology."

He smiled. "Of course, you would." He paused. "Mal has developed the ability to use Zhalto's magnetic field."

Poppy gasped.

"She's very good at it. Powerful."

"Holy cow." The thought was incredible.

"On Damar, millions died," he continued.

Poppy sucked in a breath.

"The planet was covered in wild damar-wolves. There are still many packs today. They're a sleek, small wolf. The Radiance caused a mutation that started here in Accalia. Damari and damar-wolves were somehow combined, causing the Damari infection. No one remembers exactly how it happened. It was a turbulent time, and records are sparse."

"Incredible."

"We gained strength, speed, the ability to shapeshift into a wolf. On the next planet, Taln, they can command the geological forces of the planet. I've seen my brother Graylan generate earthquakes. Collapse the ground, shoot dirt and rocks into the air."

"That sounds fascinating, but a little scary."

"Graylan is...intense." Brodin smiled. "You don't think huge wolves with large claws and volatile tempers are dangerous?"

She smiled back. "Maybe I'm getting used to it. Even Annora was nice to me today."

"But I wasn't."

She grabbed his hand. "I forgive you, Brodin. I get it. Things are pretty tense right now. Carry on with the story."

"The final planet in the system is Sarkan." His father's world. "It was unaffected by the Radiance. They rely on manufacturing weapons and vehicles of war. Zavir rules the planet with fear and intimidation."

"Oh." She shifted. "You really don't like him."

"An understatement. He is a power-hungry, *gorr*-cursed tyrant. Years ago, he tried to take over the entire system. After years of intense fighting with the planets, they proposed peace through strategic marriages. He took three wives."

"Multiple marriages? That's why he has a son on each planet."

Brodin nodded. "He wants us for our powers. He sent the warlord Krastin to Zhalto to 'convince' Rhain to join him. And he sent Candela here."

Poppy squeezed Brodin's hand. "You'll find her. You'll rescue those kids."

"I can feel the calm emanating from you." He tucked her hair behind her ear. "I'm sorry I yelled at you, Poppy. What you can do is a gift."

She laughed uncomfortably. "I'm not doing anything, Brodin. I'm bumbling around, and I hate not feeling competent."

His face turned thoughtful. "You'll find your place. You have an inner strength that is stronger than any Damari wolf I know. Now, you should rest. You need some sleep."

He started to move, but she grabbed him.

"Um, would you stay?" She shook her head and released him. "You're probably busy. You have to go. It's fine."

He gripped her chin. "I'm staying, and not just because Cassanra ordered me to keep an eye on you."

He lowered his head and kissed her.

The kiss was slow, gentle but deep.

"I shouldn't be doing this," he growled. "You're hurt, far from your world, I—"

"Shut up, Brodin." She pressed her mouth to his.

She nipped his bottom lip, and his mouth opened. Her tongue stroked his, and he took control, deepening the kiss.

"Enough," he growled, pulling back.

Poppy didn't want to stop. Every part of her was tingling.

"Sleep." He nudged her down, then lay down beside her. His big body curled around hers.

That was nice. Her heart thumped steadily. Really nice.

She felt truly safe for the first time in a long time.

She drifted off to sleep with his heartbeats in her ear, his scent filling her, and his strong arms surrounding her.

CHAPTER EIGHT

Brodin's eyes snapped open.

Someone was at his front door. He was curled around Poppy's small form. Warmth filled his chest. She'd slept soundlessly in his arms.

Gently, he touched her cheek and rose.

It was early, the sun just starting to rise over the forest. His chest locked as he wondered how Nayla and the other young ones with her were fairing.

I will find you.

He found one of his cleavers waiting on the steps, knowing Brodin would sense him.

"Emperor." Cardan bowed his head.

"Cardan."

"I have word from healer Cassanra. Fillian is awake."

A jolt went through Brodin's veins. The young man could have information on Candela, and where she was hiding.

"Brodin?" Poppy wandered out, looking sleepy and sweet.

He saw Cardan's discreet glance at Poppy's bare legs, and interest in the man's gaze.

Fighting a spurt of heat, Brodin stepped closer to her, blocking the man's view.

"Fillian is awake," he told her.

Her eyes widened. "You're going to question him?"

He nodded. "I need you to come." He didn't want to find her collapsed on the floor again.

She nodded. "I'll get dressed."

They walked quickly to the infirmary, and Cassanra met them at the door.

"Poppy, did you sleep well?" the healer asked.

She nodded.

The healer eyed Brodin with a critical eye. "You look rested too, sire."

Brodin refused to rise to the bait. "Where's Fillian?"

"Through here."

Cassanra led them down a short hall and into a comfortable healing room. It was painted in a soothing green, with lots of plants resting on shelves.

Fillian sat up in the bed. His skin was pale, and he had dark circles under his eyes. His brown hair was mussed from sleep.

"Emperor." Fillian's parents bowed their heads. They looked tired, but relief was stamped all over them.

Brodin touched their arms. "I'm glad he's fine. You need to rest now. Cassanra has him."

They nodded, and Fillian's mother kissed her son's cheek before his parents left.

"Emperor." Fillian's voice trembled.

Brodin gripped the young man's shoulder. "You're safe now."

"But Stein, Nayla, and the others aren't. My friends... That Zhylaw witch has them, and it's my fault!"

"We'll find them, and this isn't your fault. Your job now is to rest and regain your strength."

The young man's face twisted, but he nodded.

Then his gaze shifted and snagged on Poppy. The young man's face lit up. "You."

She smiled. "I'm—"

"Poppy. I remember you. You and the emperor. You made me feel better."

She looked at Brodin, then walked closer. "I'm really glad you're okay."

He reached out a hand and she took it.

"Thank you. And you, sire. For saving me."

"Fillian, we need to ask you some questions about Candela. It could help Stein and the others."

The young man's face darkened.

Brodin gently disengaged his hand from Poppy's.

"You aren't leaving, are you, Poppy?" Fillian's voice turned anxious.

"No."

Brodin urged her into a chair. "Poppy is under my protection." He met Fillian's gaze.

The young man got the message, a faint blush staining his cheekbones.

"I need you to tell me everything you remember. Nothing is too small. Any detail could help us pinpoint Candela's location."

The young man swallowed. "It's mostly a jumble. I

was hunting with Stein, and we got separated. Something hit me from behind, and knocked me out." He dragged in a deep breath. "What I remember is blurry and—" his chest hitched "—filled with pain."

His breathing quickened, and Brodin scented his fear.

Poppy pushed forward and touched Fillian's arm. Instantly, he calmed a little.

For a second, Brodin stared at her. A runa. It was simply incredible.

"I saw Candela." Fillian swallowed. "The scientists experimented on me. I remember rage and pain." His chin dropped to his chest.

"Remember that you're safe now," Poppy said.

"I..." He rubbed the side of his head, and his eyes widened. "I remember. I saw Ronmin."

"Who's that?" Poppy asked.

"One of the earlier, experienced hunters who went missing." Brodin leaned forward. "He was alive?"

"Yes, but—" Fillian swallowed. "He was screaming. They were doing things to him. Testing poisons. I heard him raging and screaming. Whatever they gave him, it drove him wild."

His eyes widened, terror filling the air.

"Fillian?" Brodin said. "Remember, you're safe."

"They gave Ronmin something. He partly changed, and he was in a rage. He got loose and...he tore a Zhylaw scientist apart."

Poppy gasped.

Brodin couldn't summon much sympathy for an

enemy who enslaved and tortured people. His own anger was a volatile simmer.

"They killed him," Fillian whispered brokenly. "All the hunters they took are dead."

Brodin bent his head, his anger exploding inside him. He fought to keep his control.

Then, as though she sensed it, Poppy brushed up against him.

The sensation of calm washed over him.

"How did you get free?" Brodin asked.

Fillian frowned. "I...I don't remember."

Cassanra walked in. "Sire, a word?"

Brodin nodded. "Fillian, rest." He turned to the healer. "When he's well enough, he needs his family, to be with his pack."

Fillian lifted his chin. "I want to help find my friends."

"I admire your loyalty, but you need to recover."

Fillian slumped back on the pillows, and gave a slow nod.

Brodin took Poppy's hand. She waved to Fillian as Brodin led her out.

Cassanra met them in the hall.

"I've tested Fillian's blood. It's filled with several synthetic poisons."

Gorr. "Are they hurting him?"

The healer shook her head. "Not now. There are only residual amounts, and eventually they'll be expelled from his system. From what I can tell, Candela is trying things to develop something perfectly designed to affect Damari physiology."

Brodin scowled, his claws pricking him. "To what? Kill us?"

"Maybe. From what I can tell, and remember, it's not my area of expertise, it drives us past our inhibitions."

"Fillian said that Ronmin was driven wild," Poppy said.

"Yes. I think the warlord is developing a chemical that drives us to pure animal," the healer said. "To rend, tear, and kill."

Brodin growled. "To turn us into rabha."

The Damari fought hard to control the wolf side of their being, to be both man and beast. As emperor, he'd executed more rabha than he cared to remember. He never forgot them.

Now, Candela wanted to drive them out of their minds. To rip each other to bloody shreds.

"I'd like to help," Poppy said. "I have some knowledge of biology and chemistry."

Testing experimental starship drives, and biology and chemistry? Brodin was starting to suspect that Poppy Ellison was a lot smarter than he'd initially guessed. "I thought your expertise was in machines."

Her cheeks went pink. "I have multiple degrees. In physics, mechanical engineering, and biology and chemistry."

"I'd appreciate any help," Cassanra said.

"All right, stay here." Brodin touched Poppy's hair and saw her lips part. He clamped down on his immediate response. "I need to check in with my cleavers and find out if the searches have turned up anything."

"Be careful," she said.

POPPY STUDIED THE BUBBLING CHEMICALS. Cassanra was nearby, poring over some scan results. Poppy really wished she could read the Damari language.

The equipment here was different, but some things followed the same principles, and Cassanra was a patient teacher. They were testing extracts from Fillian's blood, trying to isolate the poisons.

And ultimately, find ways to counteract them.

"Do you know much about this warlord Candela?" Poppy asked.

The healer's face hardened. "Only by her foul reputation. The Zhylaw have always been known for awful experiments and abusing test subjects. The hexids they sent to Zhalto are actually a peaceful species from another system. They use technology to keep them alive past their lifespans, driving them to murderous rage."

Poppy's belly cramped. "That's horrible. On Earth, we work hard to do our experiments within ethical guidelines."

"The Zhylaw have no interest in being ethical. Candela's specialty is poisons." The healer lifted a vial filled with bright green fluid.

"Why? Why do this? I can't understand the reasoning of Brodin's father."

"Zavir is driven by the belief that he, that all Sarkans, are superior. He believes that he should rule the system, and bring his version of prosperity to every part of it. He doesn't believe in free will, or choice. He doesn't care if he stifles traditions, creativity, or art."

"And all Sarkans believe this?"

Cassanra sighed. "Not all of them, but over the span of his reign, Zavir has dragged most of his people out of poverty. Instead of living on tiny, rundown farms, they have nice housing, technology, food. But in return, they have to follow his laws. He controls what they see, do, eat, sing, read, write."

"It sounds like a very plush prison."

"Yes. And he hungers to have his very, very powerful sons by his side. Not out of any sense of love of family, but as weapons."

Poppy looked back at the workbench and blinked. Her parents didn't understand her, but she never doubted that they loved her as much as they could. When she visited, her mom always made Poppy's favorite toffee. Her dad always dragged out her telescope—one they'd given her for her twelfth birthday—and they looked at the night sky together.

What would it be like to have an evil father who didn't see you, but only your power?

How could Zavir not see how incredible his son was? A fair leader who cared for his people.

"Brodin will never stop fighting Zavir. Zavir knows this, so now he's sent Candela, to poke at Brodin. To cause enough damage to Brodin to force him to Zavir's side."

"He'll never bend." Brodin was like the toughest steel.

"No. He'll protect his people."

A beep. A projection speared up with results.

Frustration hit Poppy. She really wished she could

read the notation. She'd been making her own notes on a synth pad that Cassanra had gotten for her.

Cassanra finished reading the results, then looked at Poppy. The woman smiled. "I can feel your frustration from here."

"I love reading, and gathering knowledge and facts. It's frustrating that I can't read your language."

The healer's gaze narrowed. "Wait a minute." She bustled out.

Poppy checked over their bubbling vials.

Cassanra returned, clutching a small, black device. She set it down in front of Poppy.

"What is it?" Poppy asked.

"A device we give our vision impaired." She touched a button. Light shone from the box and hit the projection Cassanra had been reading earlier. A low, female voice came from the box, talking with a slow, steady cadence.

Poppy's pulse leaped. "It reads the information aloud."

"Yes." The healer grinned. "You can use it for books, projections—"

Poppy threw her arms around the older woman. "Thank you!"

Cassanra patted her back. "You're welcome."

"Do you have any information on runas?"

"I do. It's old, and the language is quite colorful. The Damari of old fancied themselves poets."

"I don't mind."

Cassanra moved to a drawer and returned with an old, leather-bound book. "Here you go."

Poppy used her new device straight away. In between

monitoring the experiments, she pored over the information on runas.

Wolf whisperers with the ability to calm wolves. It seemed runas worked best one on one with a rabid wolf. Working with multiple out-of-control Damari was difficult, and few runas could do it without risking serious injury.

One of the bubbling vials on the bench turned a putrid black. The stench it gave off was horrible.

"I'll open a window." Poppy covered her nose and mouth with one hand. She wrenched the window open and gulped in some fresh air.

Behind her, Cassanra made a choking noise. Poppy spun. The other woman staggered and hit a workbench. Several empty vials and tools fell to the floor, smashing.

"Cassanra?" Poppy frowned.

The woman bent over, every muscle in her body straining.

"Cassanra, what's wrong?" Poppy cried.

The woman looked up. Her eyes were pure black. Her claws slashed out, her face contorted.

She snarled.

Poppy backed up. *Oh, God.*

Cassanra's gaze locked on her and she walked forward, seeming to almost grow taller.

"Cassanra, it's Poppy."

The healer stopped with a grimace, and her back arched. "P-Poppy. Get out."

Poppy straightened, continuing to move backward. "No. I can help you."

"Want... To hurt you."

"You won't. Fight it." Poppy's hip brushed the workbench, and she frantically searched through the container of medicine patches Cassanra had showed her earlier.

"Can't fight it. Too strong." The woman dropped to her knees.

Poppy found the patch she wanted and spun. She ran to Cassanra and slapped the tranquilizer on the back of the woman's neck.

Cassanra growled and slashed out, catching Poppy's arm.

Pain flashed. It was a deep cut, and blood instantly began to drip down her arm.

"Fight it, Cassanra." She touched the woman's back, and tried to project calm.

Cassanra froze, her chest heaving, and her head bowed.

She went still, but Poppy sensed her internal struggle.

The minutes ticked by, every one of them feeling like a year. Finally, Cassanra sagged, her claws retracting. She shuddered.

"Easy." Poppy helped her into a chair. "Would you like some water?"

"Yes, please." Cassanra's voice was hoarse.

Poppy poured a glass of water from a jug on a side table. She crouched and held it out.

Cassanra sipped, and eyed Poppy over the rim. "You aren't stupid, I've seen your intelligence, so you must be very brave."

"You helped me survive my transformation. I would have died without your healing. I couldn't leave you."

Cassanra grabbed Poppy's hand. "Thank you." Then she saw Poppy's bleeding forearm. "*Gorr*, let me clean that up for you. If the emperor sees it, he'll lose his mind."

Sensing the woman needed to take her mind off things, Poppy leaned against the workbench and let Cassanra clean the wound. She put a poultice on it and bandaged it. Her hands weren't fully steady yet.

"What happened?" Poppy asked.

"That poison...it did something to me. I couldn't control myself."

"Scan yourself. Let's find out what's going on."

With a nod, Cassanra did the scan and studied the results, her face set in hard lines. Poppy used her new reading device.

The healer sucked in a breath. "The poison affects the Damari brain, in the area for inhibitory control."

Poppy gasped. "It's causing you to bypass all your inhibitions."

"Yes. In the Damari, it causes homicidal, murderous tendencies. It drives the wolf out of control."

"It didn't affect me," Poppy mused.

"Maybe you didn't get a large enough dose?"

"Or because I opened the window? It diluted the effect."

"Or because you're a runa."

Lots of options, but no one answer.

"Candela is trying to perfect this," Poppy said quietly. "To infect the Damari."

Cassanra got a pinched look. "I need to run some more tests, with increased safety protocols, and then report to the emperor." She took Poppy's hand. "Thank you again, Poppy."

"You're welcome."

There was a knock at the door and Poppy's heart leaped. Maybe Brodin was back.

Annora entered. She nodded and her gaze moved to Poppy.

"Any word on your sister and the kids?" Poppy asked.

Annora's jaw worked. "Not yet. Brodin kicked me out for a bit, to clear my head." She said the last words with a growl. "Poppy, I thought you might like to train with me. To learn to utilize your new Damari abilities."

"Oh." Poppy really wanted that. "That would be great. As long as you don't beat me up in the process."

Annora's lips twitched. "I promise you'll still be walking."

"Oh, that's so reassuring."

"Good," the healer said. "I need a break. And the fresh air and exercise will do Poppy good."

"Are you sure?" Poppy asked. "I can stay and help—"

"Absolutely. Your help has been invaluable, but now I have some more work to do on that one sample."

"No testing alone."

"Of course not." Cassanra made a shooing motion with her hands. "Off you go."

CHAPTER NINE

Brodin took the twisting path through the forest. He walked up the hill, listening to the incanta birds sing. He reached the clearing, then sank down to sit. The birds continued to serenade him.

This was where his parents were buried.

The Damari burned their dead. He'd scattered their mingled ashes here. Willas had loved Brodin's mother, Jena. They'd been a true mated pair.

Not all Damari couples were mated. Some were just in love and happily joined, but sometimes, for a rare few, the bond went even beyond that. They coded to each other, generating pheromones that only attracted their mate. It was impossible for one mate to hurt, leave, or betray the other. They were linked forever.

His mother and Willas had one child together, but Brodin's tiny sister had died as a baby. He turned his head.

A small bush grew nearby, covered in pink blooms. Ember's ashes were buried beneath it.

"Hi, Mom. Hi, Willas." The man had always treated Brodin like a son. Showed him how to hunt and track. Taught him to respect females.

"I miss you both so much." He let out a harsh breath. "Zavir is causing trouble. He tried on Rhain's planet, now he's doing the same on Damar. He's taken some of our people."

His mother had been wary when Brodin had befriended Rhain and Graylan, worried they were allied with Zavir. Instead, Brodin had gained two friends, two brothers, two men he trusted.

"I will do everything I can to protect Damar and our people."

He wished for his mother's advice right now, but all he heard was the wind in the trees.

"There's a woman." In a low voice, he told them about Poppy. "She's smart, brave, cute." He shook his head. "A huge distraction. I should be focused on the fight. On the vow I made to you. On finding our lost young ones." His hands curled. "And...it hurts to care too much. Losing you both..."

It had been one of the worst days in Brodin's life. When he found out they'd died, he'd raged, gone to the forest alone for days.

"Caring for someone makes you weak," he said.

He almost heard his mother's voice. *It can also make you strong, my son.*

He heard a sound and turned his head.

Several wild damar-wolves silently padded out of the trees.

They were streamlined, with rich fur, and much

smaller than his people in their wolf forms. The damar-wolves brushed against him. They had their own alpha, but they still knew Brodin was the emperor. He stroked the sleek fur.

Then he rose. "I need to go," he said to his parents. "The trackers will be back soon, and I have to find the kids."

As always, there was no reply.

He headed back toward the main lodge. His cleavers had a small cabin and training area next door. The damar wolves followed him, sticking close.

He heard the sound of fighting from the training area. There was a large, dirt arena covered with a roof, but with open sides. He drew closer, the damar-wolves keeping pace, curious, as well.

Annora and Poppy were facing off in the center of the ring. His gut went hard.

What in the name of the wolves?

He strode forward, picking up speed.

Annora charged in. His First Claw was deadly. A few times, she'd even managed to take him down.

Poppy was no match for her.

Poppy ducked, moving surprisingly fast. She spun and landed a punch to Annora's side, before dancing back.

Annora grunted and straightened. "Nice."

"Three points to me." Poppy grinned. "I'm up to ten."

"And I have twenty," Annora said dryly.

"I can still win our bet. I really should've gotten a head start to make it fair."

"Go again, and don't get cocky."

Brodin slowed, understanding dawning in his brain.

The women attacked each other again. They traded some hits and kicks, then Annora stopped to correct Poppy's form.

On the next charge, Poppy managed to swipe Annora's legs out from under her.

"Oh, yeah." Poppy threw her arms in the air. "I'm deadly."

Brodin smiled. He decided not to mention that Annora wasn't using all her strength. His second in command rose, dusting herself off, smiling.

This was good for Poppy, and for Annora. It would help keep both of their minds off things.

At the same moment, they both scented him, and turned. The pair couldn't have been more different. One tall, fit, and dark-haired, the other small, petite, and blonde. Annora raised a brow, and Poppy smiled, wide open and beautiful.

After everything she'd been through, it was a miracle.

"Are the trackers back?" he asked.

Annora shook her head. "They found some extra clues to chase down. They should be back soon."

He nodded, frustration chewing on him.

"Cassanra and I had a breakthrough," Poppy said her face serious. "We isolated a poison from Fillian's blood. We concentrated it, and it affected Cassanra. It makes Damari lose control, have no inhibitions."

Gorr. Horror spread through him, and his jaw hardened. He traded a glance with Annora.

"If Candela can perfect that, and infect enough Damari..." Annora's voice trailed off.

It would be a bloodbath.

Damari would turn rabha and attack other Damari.

"Cassanra is running more tests," Poppy said. "The poison fades from the system over time. I don't think Candela has a working version, yet."

But she had new test subjects to experiment on until she got it right.

Until she hurt more of his people.

With a growl, he strode to the wooden post holding the roof up and punched it.

The wood cracked.

"Let's not collapse the training yard," Annora said dryly.

Poppy moved closer, her concerned gaze on him. He felt the edge of her bubble of calm.

A part of him wanted to rage, but he sucked in a few deep breaths.

"I'll check to see if there's any news on the trackers." Annora's gaze shifted between Brodin and Poppy. "Why don't you train with Poppy for a bit? Show her some moves."

His gaze narrowed. He was in no mood to spar with a woman he could snap in half. "I'm not sure—"

"She needs to learn to use all her abilities, Brodin." Annora raised her hand. "See you later, Poppy."

"Thanks, Annora." She waved back.

Clearly, Poppy had won over his First Claw.

He turned to face her, and found her gaze on the damar-wolves lounging nearby. "Gosh, they're beautiful."

"They follow me around sometimes, but they prefer the forest." He dragged in a deep breath. "Okay, let's fight."

POPPY FACED BRODIN.

God, he was so big. But she wasn't worried that he'd hurt her.

She was worried she couldn't keep her hands off that firm chest, those hard abs. She swallowed, trying to control her desire. She didn't want him scenting it.

"Show me what Annora's taught you," he said.

She nodded, then suddenly rushed him. She landed a front kick to his gut and leaped back.

Ow. It was like kicking a tree trunk.

His eyes narrowed. "Sneaky. Not bad."

He bent his legs, then he moved.

Poppy gasped and darted to evade. His fingers barely missed her. She spun and landed a chop to his side.

With a growl, he charged at her. Her adrenaline spiked and she twirled, but his hand caught the back of her shirt.

He towed her in so that her back was pressed to his front. Then he lowered his head, his mouth at her ear.

"You should be careful about getting too close to a predator, Poppy."

Her belly was alive with butterflies. Her skin flushed hot. "I know you won't hurt me."

He nipped her ear. "You sure?"

She couldn't stifle her moan.

A scent filled her senses, and she recognized her own arousal, then she picked up another deeper, scent. Masculine and mixed with spice. She jolted.

That was *his* desire.

Brodin wanted her.

"Ah, you're starting to use those Damari senses of yours." His voice was a low rumble. His big hand slid down her belly. One long finger rested right above her sex.

She bit her lip.

He was driving her crazy.

Well, two could play that game. She wiggled her butt against him, and he made a hoarse sound. Then she felt...

She swallowed. Wow, he was big. His hard cock brushed her lower back.

"I'm not as easy an opponent as Annora."

There was no boast in his voice. Just the bone-deep knowledge that he was top of the food chain around here.

She smiled and brushed against him again. His fingers tightened on her, then she moved fast, using all her new speed.

She dropped and swiped out her leg, like Annora had showed her.

She clearly surprised Brodin, as he went down hard.

Grinning, she leaped and straddled his legs. "Look who's flat on his back now."

He smiled.

It didn't soften his rugged face, but some of the lines of tension around his mouth eased. She liked that. Liked knowing that she—boring, smart Poppy Ellison—could help this big, wild alien king relax a little.

His hands gripped her hips. "Nice move, Poppy."

With a tug, he pulled her up his body so that she straddled his hips.

She gasped. That big, hard bulge was right at the juncture of her thighs.

She was instantly drenched.

He groaned. "You smell so good, Poppy. It makes me wonder how you'll taste."

"*Brodin*." She heard the need in her own voice.

With a flex of muscles, he sat up, so they were face to face and his mouth took hers.

Oh, God. The wild flavor of him hit her like an explosion.

The kiss was hard, fierce, and filled with savage possession. His tongue stroked hers and she made a sound, winding her arms around him. She melted against him.

Poppy shimmied, pure sensation shooting through her. Desire exploded low in her belly.

He made a hungry noise, part growl, part groan.

Something went off inside of Poppy. She'd never wanted anyone like this, never been wanted like this.

She pressed into that hard chest and kissed him harder. She wanted more, needed more. His mouth traveled down the side of her neck.

Oh. She arched and writhed against him, sensation swirling low. The movement brushed against her clit and felt so good. His hands were on her hips, urging her on.

Then his mouth reached where her neck met her shoulder.

Growling, he bit her.

Poppy jerked against him and came. She cried out, her body shuddering as intense pleasure washed over her.

She opened her eyes.

His burned with an inner fire. Brodin—this big, gorgeous, powerful king—wanted her.

"I want to bite you," she panted.

God. Had those words really come out of her?

His eyes flashed. Then, he tilted his head.

She stared at his skin, her heart thumping hard in her chest. All that beautiful bronze skin. She leaned close and sniffed him—such a sexy, earthy male scent.

Her belly tightened. She was turned on again. She peppered kisses over his salty skin.

He let out a low groan.

She scraped her teeth over his neck, felt his pulse beating under his skin.

She bit him.

His body jolted. "*Poppy*."

His hand tangled in her hair, and he tugged her mouth to his. His tongue stroked hers, the kiss raw and powerful. Poppy wanted him—desperately.

Right there, right now.

Suddenly, Brodin tensed, his mouth lifting off hers.

Dazed, Poppy blinked. *No*. She wanted to drag his mouth back to hers. She followed his gaze.

A man was standing nearby, studiously looking away from them. He was muscled and strong, and she guessed he was probably one of Brodin's cleavers.

Brodin sighed and pushed up, lifting her with him.

"We'll finish this later," he murmured. He stroked his thumb over her lips.

She couldn't help herself. She nipped his thumb and saw that gold sheen roll over his eyes.

"You tempt my wolf, Poppy Ellison."

She'd never tempted anyone before.

She liked it.

He took her hand. "Luka."

The man turned and lowered his gaze. "Emperor."

"What is it?"

"A tracker came in from Pennata. He saw the warlord Candela."

Poppy gasped.

Brodin stiffened. "Where?"

"Close to Kalmia, sire."

Brodin looked at Poppy. "A small town an hour north of Accalia."

"She was with several Zhylaw, and moving away from the city," Luka added.

Poppy felt a prick of unease.

Candela was moving away from the city? What had she been doing here in the first place?

"All right, find Annora, and call a meeting with the cleavers," Brodin ordered.

The man snapped to attention and nodded. "Yes, sire."

Then both men tensed. Poppy heard someone running in their direction.

She turned and saw Annora sprinting at full speed, her long legs moving fast.

"Brodin!" Annora's eyes were wide. "There's a fight in the city. In the market."

"Who's attacking?"

"No one." Annora shook her head. "Our people are rampaging. The citizens of Accalia are fighting each other."

CHAPTER TEN

Brodin's blood fired.

Candela. She'd caused this.

"Poppy, stay here."

She lifted her chin. "No. I might be able to help."

He ground his teeth together. Her cheeks were still flushed from what they'd been doing before. But the hard, stubborn glint in her eye said she wasn't going to budge.

Gorr.

"Let's go. Stay close." He looked over Poppy's head and met Annora's gaze.

Look out for her.

His First Claw nodded.

They moved into a jog, Luka with them. As they neared the marketplace, he heard shouts, growls, screams, and things crashing.

His gut hardened, and his claws sliced out.

He picked up speed and turned the corner.

Stalls were overturned, the square was littered with

broken and damaged goods, and Damari were fighting. A few were in wolf form, the rest in a part shift, with their claws slashing. Some people were curled on the ground, bleeding.

Brodin threw his head back and howled. Then he looked at Poppy, already feeling his wolf tugging at him, desperate to enter the fight and save his people.

"Poppy, stay back."

She nodded, her face pale as she took in the destruction. "Go."

He, Annora, and Luka raced into the fight. Brodin tore two fighters apart, tossing them aside. He saw a crying child in the midst of the chaos.

Brodin charged in, knocking a wolf aside, and leaped over a broken, overturned stall.

He scooped up the crying girl.

"E-Emperor," she sobbed.

"You're okay now." He ran to a nearby closed doorway and thumped his fist on it.

The door cracked open, and the eye of a frightened woman looked through. She saw the girl and nodded. "I'll take her."

"Stay inside." He handed the girl over. "Keep the door locked."

He whirled. People were screaming and slashing at each other.

His people.

He waded back into the mêlée. He could see his people's eyes were flooded with black, and they looked crazed, out of their minds. He pulled one of his off-duty cleavers off another man.

"Rasso!" Brodin roared.

The man's eyes were glazed. He snarled, twisting and jerking. Brodin punched him and knocked him out. There was something very wrong with them.

He saw Annora fighting two out-of-control storeowners. She kicked one, then slammed the other one to the ground.

Luka was trying to subdue another man. The rest of the cleavers arrived, wading into the fight.

Movement above caught Brodin's gaze, and he looked up.

Poppy was on top of one of the stalls. She leaped from one to the other, graceful.

What in the gorr *was she doing?*

A woman rushed at him, her hair wild and loose, fangs bared.

He grabbed her and spun her, wrapped his arms around her. She twisted and snapped. Her claws bit into his forearms.

Brodin grasped the side of her neck and found a pressure point. She collapsed, and he gently set her down.

Even with all his cleavers, they were heavily outnumbered. More wild, rampaging people stormed out of the heart of the market.

Gorr. They couldn't safely take them all down.

But they had to try.

He charged into the center of the mob. Brodin whirled and ducked. When he could, he knocked several people out.

A large, brown wolf leaped over the downed people, aiming for Brodin's throat.

He grabbed the beast. He recognized the markings—the white patch of fur on the tail, the golden glow of light in the fur.

Senya was a weaponsmith in the market. Friendly, bubbly.

She snarled, and tried for Brodin's throat again. He gripped her and spotted a chain nearby. He snatched it and wrapped it around the wolf's neck.

Senya snarled and yanked futilely.

Brodin felt the slash of claws on his back. He blocked the pain and turned. In seconds, he'd knocked out the attacking Damari. Brodin rushed back into the chaos.

He spotted Annora, her face bleeding. She tossed a man into a wall.

"We can't keep this up," she yelled.

"If they get loose, they'll tear through the city." Brodin punched a man in the gut, then planted a chop to his back.

He took more hits, but he got two more of them down.

He looked up and spotted Poppy. She was up on a ledge, but focused on the heart of the fighting crowd.

What was she doing?

Brodin saw a man closest to her spot her. The man slowed to a stop and stared at her.

She was using her runa ability.

Brodin's chest hitched. There were too many. She'd burn herself out.

Another three people ran at him, their faces twisted and screaming.

Suddenly, Poppy leaped off the ledge...right into the center of the wild crowd.

No. "Poppy!"

Brodin charged forward, shouldering people out of his way. His pulse raced wildly.

She'd be trampled, or torn to shreds. He *had* to get to her.

He heard Annora curse, fighting her way toward him.

He couldn't lose Poppy. Not now.

Then he saw several raging people just...sit down.

They looked dazed, blinking, confused. Some started to cry. All around, the fighting Damari stopped. Most were pale, and looked as though they were shaking off a bad dream.

"Emperor?" A man looked at him blankly. "What happened?"

"I remember," a woman sobbed. "Rage. Terrible rage. I couldn't think. All I wanted to do was slash and destroy." Tears rolled down her face.

"Sit down and take a breath." He scanned for Poppy.

More people dropped to the ground, shell-shocked. A few were rocking, and a few others hugged each other.

Then he saw Poppy rise. Her clothes were torn, and she had a smear of blood on her cheek.

"Poppy!" He pushed toward her.

She was impossibly pale, her face drained.

"I'm...trying to help them." Her voice wavered.

As he got closer, he felt a rush of calm. "Everyone's stopped fighting, you can let go now."

She bit her lip, nodded. The sensation of calm slowly started to dissipate.

The Damari seemed okay, but many were slumped on the ground.

Brodin met her gaze.

She'd done it. She'd stopped a massacre.

She gave him a wobbly smile.

Then what little color was in her face drained away and she started to collapse.

No. He charged across the last of the distance to her and pulled her into his arms.

Frantically, he felt for a pulse. He found it strong and steady.

"Annora?" he roared.

"Yes." She appeared at his side.

"Get Cassanra and the healers. *Now.*"

POPPY FOUGHT through the fog in her head. She felt someone holding her and she felt so tired, drained. Like she'd been out running on a hot, summer day. Her throat was parched.

She opened her eyes.

Brodin's stony face came into view.

"Hey." She cupped his cheek.

His gaze locked on her, and his scowl deepened. "Next time you jump into a wild, rampaging crowd, I'll spank you."

Her mouth dropped open. Mainly because the idea frankly didn't bother her very much. She cleared her throat. "Is everyone okay?"

"Three people are dead. More are injured, but the healers are helping them."

She turned her head. She was snuggled in Brodin's lap. He was sitting on a table located on the edge of the marketplace. Cleavers were patrolling the edges, and healers were moving between the victims.

God.

It had been so horrible, seeing the citizens of Accalia tearing each other apart.

She felt rage throbbing off Brodin, but she didn't do anything to try and calm him.

He'd apologized about his outburst the last time, but the hurt was still sharp in her mind. Poppy knew that sometimes you had to feel the bad emotions to appreciate the good ones, to live life to the fullest.

His hands tightened on her. She turned her head into his neck. She saw the small mark she'd left when she'd bitten him and her belly heated. She pressed her face to his skin.

Brodin blew out a breath and rested his face on her hair.

She stayed like that, and she thought it helped him, but she still felt his anger and sorrow like a growing storm.

Cassanra headed their way. There were lines on the healer's face, and she looked exhausted.

"Emperor."

"Cassanra."

The healer sighed, her hands clenched in her skirt. "Another died. Marth. He ran a leather goods store. Two more are gravely injured, and I am not sure they'll survive the night. We'll do our best."

"Candela did this," he growled.

"Yes. I did preliminary scans. They're all carrying the toxin in their blood. I need to do more detailed tests, but I suspect it is a version of what Poppy and I isolated from Fillian."

"How? How did she infect so many?"

Cassanra spread her hands. "I don't know."

"It's not airborne," Poppy said. "Brodin, Annora, and I were not affected when we arrived."

Cassanra frowned. "I don't know for certain. Yet."

"Poppy leaped into the crowd and calmed them." His voice vibrated with unrestrained anger.

Ah, he wasn't quite ready to let that go yet. "I couldn't let them hurt each other."

"She collapsed," Brodin said.

Cassanra lifted her scanner. Poppy rolled her eyes and sat through it.

"I've been reading more on runa," the healer said. "Calming a crowd is difficult. It is not a common skill."

"I wasn't even sure it would work. I still don't understand this ability."

Brodin growled. "You didn't know if it would work, and you still jumped in there?"

She glared at him. "I had to try."

"You could've been killed!"

"I wasn't."

"You release some sort of pheromone," Cassanra said.

Poppy blinked. "What?"

"Runa skills appear to be similar to a mated pair,

except in that instance, their pheromones only work on each other. Runas could emit pheromones that affect all Damari in a calming way."

"Oh." A horrible thought occurred. She tried to scramble off Brodin, but he held her tight. "Is that why—?" She swallowed, her heart beating hard. "Is that why Brodin...?"

She couldn't voice her worry. His heavy arm slid around her, his mouth at her ear. "No."

That deep voice was a growl.

Was he attracted to her because she exuded some pheromone?

Cassanra smiled, knowingly. "Is that why the emperor's attracted to you? No. You only emit calming pheromones when you actively use your ability. The rest of the time, you're all you."

Poppy sagged against him.

He caressed her hip.

"We'll finish up and get the injured back to the infirmary," Cassanra said.

"Cassanra, find out how Candela did this," Brodin growled. "We have to find a way to stop it from happening again."

The woman gave him a brisk nod. "I won't stop until I do." She looked at them both. "You two should get some rest."

"I need to check on everyone first." Brodin set Poppy down on the table beside him.

She watched him stalk off, and have a quick word with a female cleaver, then he moved through the crowd.

She saw the way the people looked at him for

strength. He cupped cheeks, patted shoulders, hugged people. He was a good king, the leader they trusted and looked up to.

She saw the female cleaver he'd spoken to shift closer to Poppy.

She felt a brief burst of annoyance mixed with pleasure. He was looking out for her. *Again.*

Poppy wrapped her arms around her knees and watched him give so much comfort. People absorbed his strength.

And he took all of their pain, their struggles, on those broad shoulders.

But she saw the strain, the tension. Did no one else?

Finally, he made his way back to her.

His jaw was tight, his eyes boiling. She felt the swelling rage.

He held out a big hand, and she took it and jumped off the table.

They walked back toward his cabin in silence. She felt an urge to help him welling. It almost hurt to hold back, and she bit her lip.

Then, he led her inside his cabin, straight to the huge, tan couch in his living area, and he dropped down.

He pulled her onto his lap. This seemed to be his favorite spot for her. His big body was so tense. She stroked his shoulder.

"Candela will die," he said.

"You'll stop her." Poppy fingered that thick, silver-white hair of his. She toyed with one of the braids at his temple. She felt her calm seep out of her, and she fought to hold it back.

It hurt, and she let out a small whimper.

He lifted her chin up.

"Your eyes are gold," he said. "You want to soothe me."

"I know you didn't like it, so—"

"Don't hold back. I'm sorry about my reaction the first time. I understand it's a part of you, part of you and your Damari abilities." He stroked her jaw. "I was an ass before. Do it."

The sensation flooded out of her, and she let out a sigh of relief. She saw him relax, his pupils contracting. He let out a long sigh.

Then he tucked her under his chin. "Thank you."

"Just hold me," she murmured.

"I will."

CHAPTER ELEVEN

The next morning, Brodin once again headed out to meet his cleavers. He hoped they had better news for him today.

Poppy was with him.

Rage for Candela and his father was still inside him, but now coated with a layer of control. A night spent wrapped around Poppy had helped.

She'd tended the scratches he'd gotten in the fight, both of them excruciatingly aware of the growing desire between them. Then Annora and some of his cleavers had arrived with updates on the trackers, and all of them looking for reassurance from their emperor. Tolf was holding onto his rage and worry for his brother by a thread.

Brodin was conscious that it was another night that Nayla, Stein, and the other teens had been gone.

Whatever he had to do to stop the warlord hurting more of his people, he'd do it.

Annora and the others were in the cleaver lodge. His

First Claw was brewing a pot of cinnamae. She smiled, but looked tense.

He knew she was worried about her sister.

Brodin gripped her shoulder. "Don't lose hope."

Annora nodded. "Poppy, have you tried cinnamae?"

Poppy shook her head.

Annora gave her a mug, and she took a tentative sip.

"Mmm, it's not like anything on Earth. I like it." She sipped it again.

Watching her eat and drink made Brodin happy. Knowing she enjoyed discovering everything about Damar pleased him.

The doors opened and Cassanra appeared. The healer wore leather pants and a green, smock-style shirt.

Brodin stiffened. "The injured?"

"Healing well."

His chest loosened a little. Good. He didn't want to lose more people.

"I think I know how Candela infected the people in the market," the healer said.

"Did they ingest it?" Poppy asked.

Cassanra shook her head. She touched her projecta band and blue text shot up.

"Several of the injured from the market said a swarm of rockflies flew through prior to the fight."

"Rockflies?" Poppy frowned.

"Insects," Brodin told her. "Annoying insects. They're not harmful, but their bites itch."

"Ah, we have something similar on Earth called mosquitoes."

"The swarm flew through, then disappeared." Images

appeared on the healer's projection. "All the people who are infected had bites." Images of small welts appeared.

Poppy gasped and nodded. "Candela used the rock-flies to deliver the poison."

Brodin scowled. He hated the Zhylaw. "Is there any way to stop this happening again? A way to protect ourselves?"

Cassanra's mouth tightened. "I'll work on something, but I haven't got anything yet."

"So don't get bitten," Poppy said.

The doors burst open. A mud-splattered tracker, Darther, ran inside.

"Sire! I saw Candela with a crew of Zhylaw. To the north, near Brierra Lake."

Brodin straightened. Close. *Too close.* Brierra Lake was a water source for the city.

He spun. "Annora, assemble a team. We'll take two drifters to the lake."

His First Claw nodded and turned, shouting out orders.

Poppy stepped forward. "I'm coming."

"No." It was too dangerous. Every protective instinct in his body revolted at the thought.

"Brodin, how many times are we going to have this argument? If Candela infects any of you, I'm the only antidote you have."

His jaw worked. He cursed. "Fine. But I'm assigning a cleaver to you. You'll stay by their side."

She nodded.

The cleavers opened the weapons lockers lining the back of the room. They all changed into their leather armor and grabbed their weapons—staffs, clubs, axes. Annora pulled out her favorite club. Crafted for her, it had a carved hilt, and a strong, sturdy design.

Brodin pulled out his axe and strapped it to his back. They could all fight with their claws or in wolf form, but they weren't just the wolf. All of them trained with multiple weapons. A semi shift was the preferred fighting form. It allowed them more dexterity and the ability to talk, all while using their claws and strength.

Then he opened the locker that stored the spare armor and weapons. He pulled out the smallest leather vest he could find.

"I want you to wear this." He held it out to Poppy.

She turned and he helped her fit it over her shirt, and tightened the straps. It was a little too big, but would give her mid-section decent protection.

"Let's move."

The drifters were rugged, open-topped vehicles designed for the forest, with solar-powered engines. They climbed in, Annora claiming the driver's seat with Brodin beside her. Poppy sat in the back, sitting between two cleavers who dwarfed her.

"Luka, Poppy is your first priority."

"Yes, Emperor," the shaggy-haired man replied.

Annora started the engine. The vehicle was nearly silent. She grasped the U-shaped controller in front of her and they pulled out. A second drifter followed behind them.

They followed the track into the trees. Brierra Lake was an hour drive away.

"What's our plan?" Annora asked, as she kept the vehicle on the track.

"Stop before the lake and go in on foot."

His First Claw nodded.

They reached the parking area and climbed out.

"We need to move fast and silently," Brodin told them.

Poppy lifted her chin, looking determined.

They set off, jogging through the trees.

Soon, Brodin scented the lake, and the intruders. The faint chemical smell of the Zhylaw.

He held up his fist, and his cleavers stopped. They dropped to their bellies and shimmied forward.

The water of Brierra Lake gleamed like a jewel. It provided crisp, clear water to the city and was monitored by the science teams. Brodin scanned the tree line. An owna hawk made large, wheeling circles in the sky. They were always interested and curious, so he zeroed in under it.

"To the right," he said. "Twenty cora from the lake."

"I see them," Annora murmured.

Several Zhylaw stood by the water. They were all slender, of medium height, and clothed in stark, black uniforms. The sunlight glinted off two black vehicles. They were simple in design, with a flat bed at the back for hauling things.

Then, a woman with red-and-black hair stepped out of the trees.

She was curvy for a Zhylaw, wearing a black, all-in-one suit. Her hair whipped around her face like it was alive. It was rumored that the ends were tipped with poison. She wore metallic gloves whose fingers ended in claw-like spikes.

"That's her?" Poppy's voice held disdain.

"That's her."

Large, pod-like canisters rested on the back of the vehicles. He needed to know what they were.

"Let's get closer. Keep an eye out for any sign of our people."

His group moved quietly. It was unlikely the Zhylaw would detect them. They weren't hunters or predators like the Damari. They relied on their tech, not their senses.

They got closer, and he heard the murmur of conversation.

"Zavir wants his son. Everyone else is expendable." Candela smiled darkly, her voice sharp. "The rest we'll watch act like the animals they are."

"Yes, Warlord."

"For now, we wait," Candela said.

"Our drone from the city showed that the Damari managed to avert the massacre," a male Zhylaw scientist in a black uniform said.

Candela smile's slipped, her hair waving across her face. "A minor setback."

The Zhylaw shrugged. "King Zavir isn't fond of setbacks, Candela." The man sounded smug.

Candela's gaze narrowed to the man, and she cocked her head. "Are you angling for my job, Gav?"

The man lifted his chin. "If you can't get Emperor Sarkany to join his father, then I'm happy to try."

Candela's smile turned scary, and she sauntered

closer. "I don't fail." She moved fast and ran her claw-tipped fingers into the man's gut. "And I can't be replaced."

The man choked. She stepped back and he clutched his bleeding stomach. Black blood spread over his skin. He made a panicked sound.

"A new version of my tasseloris agent." She smiled. "I'm told the poison's effects are excruciatingly painful."

The man screamed. His skin turned black, and it spread, climbing up his neck. His skin cracked in places. He collapsed, convulsing on the ground, and making horrible noises.

Poppy looked away. Brodin touched her back.

Enough.

He'd stop Candela. *Now.*

He rose, his cleavers with him.

Luka grabbed Poppy's arm to hold her back.

Brodin put her out of his mind, and stepped out of the trees.

Candela spun. "Ah, you've arrived. I knew you would."

"I've come to kill you," Brodin said.

She gave a throaty laugh. "You aren't strong enough, or smart enough, Emperor."

"My claws cut a lot better than your fake ones."

A smile flirted around her mouth, and she lifted one hand. Her metal claws glinting in the sunlight.

"Release the rockflies," Candela yelled.

Two Zhylaw near the vehicles opened the pods.

Insects streamed out.

POPPY STARED in horror as the insects streamed into the air. They dipped and weaved, moving as one.

Brodin, Annora, and the cleavers focused on Candela and the Zhylaw, as though the insects weren't even there.

But if they got bitten...

Pulse racing, Poppy surged up, but Luka pulled her back down.

"We have to help," she said.

The cleaver's jaw was tight. "We have to wait."

Brodin focused on Candela. He let out a howl that raised goose bumps on Poppy's arms. Brodin and his cleavers charged, drawing their weapons.

The cleavers cut down several Zhylaw.

Brodin went after Candela. The warlord pulled a long piece of rope off her belt. It glowed red, clearly full of energy.

A whip.

She snapped it at Brodin. It curled around his forearm, and he hissed. His huge axe fell to the ground. The warlord yanked back, and Poppy stared in horror at the burn on his arm.

She glanced up to check on the insects. They were wheeling around in circles in the sky. She knew they'd swarm at any moment.

Zhylaw screamed, and the Damari growled.

The rockflies arrowed downward.

"Watch out!" Poppy shouted.

Candela's head jerked up, and she looked right at Poppy.

The Damari all dropped flat.

The insects soared overhead and flocked around a Zhylaw man. He slapped at them.

Brodin leaped up and collided with Candela.

The other Damari attacked and took down more Zhylaw.

The insects moved over the lake and then flew back. Poppy saw them hit two cleavers. The man and woman dropped, their backs arching.

Oh, no.

They snarled and attacked the other cleavers.

Poppy ripped free of Luka. "I have to help them."

She sprinted forward, toward the fighting cleavers.

Annora saw her. "Poppy!"

Poppy flung her arms out. The sense of calm hit the infected cleavers and they jerked. They stopped, panting hard.

Nearby, Candela broke free from Brodin and leaped on top of a vehicle.

She glared at Poppy. "What are you?"

Brodin growled and stalked the warlord, his claws out.

"*Gorr*, they're coming back," a cleaver yelled.

"To me," Poppy yelled.

The cleavers surrounded her. The rockflies swarmed them all.

Poppy felt the brush of the tiny bodies and the sting of bites.

"*Gorr*," a cleaver cried.

Then the insects passed by.

"Is everyone okay?" Poppy asked.

"Yes." Annora turned. "We have to help Brodin."

He was on the roof of the vehicle. Candela was bleeding, but had her whip wrapped around him, burning him. The scent of seared skin filled the air.

He slashed one hand down, his claws slicing Candela's whip in half. He leaped back. With a roar he charged her, tackling her off the vehicle.

"We have to find a way to stop the rockflies," Poppy said.

"How?" Luka asked.

She looked around. They were close to the second Zhylaw vehicle, and she felt a faint throb of energy off it.

Her mind ticked over.

"Look out!" Annora yelled.

Two Zhylaw held up a weapon of some sort. It whined, and let loose with a pulse of energy. Annora rammed into Poppy, tackling her to the ground. Cleavers leaped up and charged the Zhylaw.

"Oh, *gorr*." There was horror in Annora's voice.

Poppy looked up.

She saw the insects swarm Brodin. Her chest locked.

No. *No*.

His back bowed. His claws grew longer, and the bones in his face shifted. He let out a snarl.

Candela laughed.

"He'll kill us all," Annora whispered.

Poppy wriggled free and ran at him.

"Poppy!" Annora yelled.

Brodin heard her. His eyes were pure gold and she

saw him straining to control himself. She leaped at him and hit his chest. She wrapped her arms and legs around him.

"Brodin. *Brodin.*" She put everything she could into him.

He opened his jaw. His teeth were longer.

"Stop it," she snapped.

Brodin blinked. Blue bled back into his eyes.

"Poppy?" His voice was a hoarse rasp.

"Yes." She stroked his cheek. "Fight it off."

"Just what are you?" Candela snapped.

Brodin smiled, his hands tightening on Poppy.

"You're ruining everything," the warlord spat.

"Get used to it," Poppy said. "I'm not going to let you get away with hurting anyone else."

Brodin set Poppy down and advanced on Candela.

The warlord's eyes widened. Her red-and-black hair snapped out, moving like water. It touched his skin and Poppy watched green spots appear.

With a hiss, he jerked back.

"Give me the woman and I'll leave you alone, Emperor," Candela said.

"No," he growled.

"I want her. I won't let her ruin my plans."

"Brodin, look out," Annora cried.

Poppy saw the rockflies coming back, buzzing madly.

Candela dove behind the vehicle. Brodin grabbed Poppy and they hit the ground. He rolled them under the vehicle.

"We have to stop those bugs," she said.

"How?"

She looked up at the bottom of the Zhylaw vehicle.

"Let's see what we have here." She pried a panel off. Brodin pulled more off for her.

Shouts echoed from beyond the vehicle, but she tried to focus. Her pulse was racing. The insects were after the cleavers.

She focused on the guts of the vehicle. There were wires, and other weird things. *Shit.* Nothing looked familiar. "Do you know how these are powered?"

"Electromagnetic cells. Here." He pulled another panel free.

A glowing cube sat in the newly revealed space.

Hmm. Yes, she saw how it worked. She yanked wires out, connected and fiddled.

"Don't touch the body of the vehicle," she warned.

A humming noise filled her ears, and energy pumped into the air. The hairs rose on her body.

"Now we need to lure the rockflies to us."

Brodin nodded and rolled out from under the vehicle. He waved his arms.

The bugs wheeled around and flew toward him.

Then, like hitting an invisible wall, they stopped. They smacked into the energy field coming off the vehicle and dropped to the ground. They rained down like ash.

Brodin picked one up. "Dead."

Poppy killed the field and climbed out.

He smiled. "You're a genius." Then he lowered his head and kissed her.

Breathless, she smiled back, then frowned. "Where's Candela?"

Brodin scowled. "Where the *gorr* did she go?"

Annora strode to them, her face covered in small, bleeding bites. "Candela escaped."

CHAPTER TWELVE

Brodin stomped through the trees carrying the injured Tolf.

The man had been hurt by the energy pulse. Tolf was gritting his teeth and sweating.

"Not much farther to the drifters, Tolf."

"I can make it, Emperor. I'm not too bad."

"You're a terrible liar."

The man gave him a thin smile.

Poppy walked beside him. Her clothes were streaked with dirt, and her hair was loose.

She was fine.

She'd saved them.

She was so clever, his small woman from Earth.

Annora was nearby, walking with her arm around another injured cleaver.

Brodin was furious that Candela had escaped. He sucked in a breath. Still, they'd won this battle.

The warlord would need to regroup, but now she knew about Poppy.

Poppy would be her next target.

Gorr, his father was to blame. Brodin hated Zavir.

They reached the drifters and loaded everyone in. Brodin climbed into the driver's seat of one vehicle, Annora the other. Poppy sat beside him, eyeing all the controls with interest. Give her some tools, and he suspected she'd have the vehicle pulled apart in minutes.

Brodin drove, his mind churning with thoughts of Candela, until they reached the edge of Accalia. He headed straight to the infirmary.

Cassanra was waiting for them. She eyed the injured as they climbed out of the drifters. "Inside," she ordered.

Brodin set Tolf on a bunk. The other cleavers put the rest of the injured in other rooms.

The healer looked Brodin up and down. "Are you injured?"

"I'm fine. Take care of Tolf."

Cassanra raised a brow. "Poppy?"

"I'm fine, too."

The healer gave them a look, but nodded. "Any sign of the children?"

"No." His frustration burned through his bloodstream. "And Candela got away."

"But we roasted her cloud of infected rockflies," Poppy said.

The healer's eyebrows rose. "She won't be happy about that."

No. Brodin's hand flexed. She'd be looking for revenge.

"There is nothing more you can do this afternoon.

You all need a good rest. You can't help the children if you're exhausted."

Brodin took Poppy's hand. Annora was waiting for them outside.

"Double night patrols," he said.

His First Claw nodded. "Good idea."

He noted the dark circles under his friend's eyes. "You're tired."

"I'm not sleeping well. I can't stop thinking of Nayla. Wondering if she's scared."

Brodin pulled her to his chest, and heard her sigh. "Nayla will be waiting for her sister to come and get her. Now rest. That's an order."

Annora gave a tight nod. "Thanks, Brodin. Poppy."

Poppy was quiet as they headed to his cabin. He could almost hear her thinking.

"What's on your mind, Dr. Ellison?"

"Candela wants me."

His gut twisted. "She's not getting you."

She squeezed his fingers. "But you could use this to your advantage."

Tension filled him. He didn't like where this was headed.

"You need to lure her out, so you can find the kids—"

His gut cramped. "Poppy."

She faced him. "Use me. I can be bait, and—"

With a low roar, he spun and stalked away. His hands curled into fists.

"It makes sense, Brodin."

He spun back. "No."

She drew herself up, but was still so tiny. So breakable.

"Yes. We'll plan it out and—"

He gave another roar, dipped, and tossed her over his shoulder.

She gasped. "Brodin!"

The sun was headed toward the horizon, and he stalked through the late afternoon glow. They passed several Damari on the path, all watching the unfolding action with undisguised interest.

"Brodin, put me down," she hissed.

"I'm the Emperor of Damar. I give the commands." He slapped a hand on her small, curvy butt. They reached his cabin, but he circled around it. He needed privacy for all the things he wanted to do to Poppy Ellison.

She'd tipped his world upside down. She was courageous, with an inner strength he admired.

She was willing to risk herself for children she didn't even know.

"Where are you taking me?"

"Somewhere private." His own private lair that he didn't share with anyone. It was his own hideaway for when he needed time to be alone.

But he wanted her there.

He made his way through the trees, the forest sounds changing as the animals prepared for the incoming night.

Finally, they broke out of the tree line. A tall column of rock, with greenery growing and dripping over the side, rose up above the trees.

He circled the back of it and reached the locked doorway. He opened the lock and walked up the circular stairs.

At the top, he set Poppy down, then lit some lanterns.

She looked around, her mouth dropping open.

The room was carved from the rock. A large, window-like opening, covered by an overhang that let no rain in, faced the forest. A large, metal tub was tucked against one wall, sized for him, so it was big. In the other corner was a large bed that sat low to the floor. It was covered with fur blankets.

Galliosa draped from the walls and the vine smelled rich and green.

"What is this place?" she asked.

"My little hideaway. My lair."

She wandered around, and her hand touched the edge of the tub. She eyed the pile of books resting by his bed. A rock shelf built into the wall held some mechanica —several wolves on the hunt.

"This is your sanctuary."

He shrugged. "Being emperor, my people need me. I don't mind that..."

"But sometimes you need to get away." She glanced around. "Sit in your big tub and read a book."

That was exactly what he did.

She turned to the window.

It gave a perfect view of the forest, and Accalia nestled in the trees. The sun was setting, and some stars were appearing in the sky overhead, including a pretty nebula.

"Your planet is stunning, Brodin."

He came up behind her. "You haven't seen all of it.

The ice forests to the south. The Asari grasslands. The Duranti sea, with waters bluer than your eyes."

He lowered his head and sniffed her neck.

She shivered.

"You cold?"

"No."

He ran his hands down her arms. "I'm going to have you now, Poppy. Finally discover how you taste."

She tilted her head, and he raked his teeth down her neck.

"Oh, God." She pushed back against him.

"Is that what you want?" His voice was guttural.

"Yes." Her voice held a growl. A sheen of gold glittered over her eyes.

He stepped back and started to shed his clothes. He walked to the tub and pulled the handle. Warm water splashed into it.

Naked, he stepped into it and dropped into place. He rested his arms along the top edge.

When he looked back up, Poppy was skimming her pants down to uncover her slim legs. Then she pulled her shirt off.

Moonlight hit her, and his cock throbbed. Slim, petite, and gorgeous.

She walked toward him, and he sensed her nerves and desire.

"Get in the tub, Poppy. I want you to straddle me so I can suck your pretty breasts."

She drew in a breath. "Brodin..."

"They're so lovely, topped with those pebbled pink nipples."

Her chest hitched, but she stepped into the tub. He saw the fascinating flash of gold curls at the juncture of her thighs, the smooth curve of her belly, the slim thighs he wanted wrapped around his hips.

Yes, tonight, he'd have his sweet, succulent woman from Earth.

SHE STEPPED INTO THE TUB, warm water lapping at her knees.

But all Poppy could see was Brodin.

Big, muscled, hard Brodin.

He sat there, like the alien king he was, water and shadows doing a bad job of hiding his massive erection.

She swallowed, heat clawing at her belly. She moved closer, aware of his hot gaze lazily perusing her body. One arm lifted and he curled it around her. His big palm cupped her butt, caressed.

She bit her lip.

He tugged her closer. God, he was eye level with her belly.

"Straddle me," he ordered.

She bent her knees, sinking on top of him. Her heart was pounding so hard.

His huge cock brushed between her legs, and she let out a soft moan. "Um, Brodin, I want you to know that I have an implant. It prevents pregnancy."

His eyes flashed. "Okay."

"What about...sexually transmitted diseases?"

He frowned. "We have no such things among the

Damari."

She smiled and rocked her hips. "Good."

With a growl, he took her mouth.

His fingers curled around her neck, holding her in place for the sensual onslaught. His tongue thrust into her mouth, and she kissed him back. She couldn't hold still. She gripped his muscular shoulders, hips moving, sliding that tantalizing cock against her.

He pulled his head back. "You are so beautiful, Poppy." He lowered his head and sucked her nipple into his mouth. "So sweet."

"You're so gorgeous." Oh, his mouth felt so good. Everything he did caused sensation to arrow straight between her legs. "No one's ever wanted me like you do."

"Then the men of the Earth are idiots."

Brodin took his time, tongue toying with her nipple. Her back bowed, small cries escaping her. Her hips jerked as he nibbled at her, sending water sloshing against the side of the tub. He switched to her other breast. She slid her hands into his unbound silver-white hair.

Then her fingers ran over his chest. She needed to hold on to him to stay anchored or she'd fly apart.

He lifted his head, then his mouth was back on hers. He kissed her—deep, drugging kisses.

One of his hands drifted down to her belly, and one finger dipped into her belly button, then he delved between her thighs.

Poppy cried out and lifted her hips. He stroked her, then thrust a thick finger inside her.

Oh, God.

"Tight, my sweet Poppy. You'll feel my cock when I slide inside you."

Her lips parted. "*Brodin.*"

His finger plunged in and out, then he brushed her clit. She jerked.

"Ah, here's what I'd hoped to find."

She panted as he rolled her clit. "Damari women are—?"

"Similar." He pinched the swollen nub and she moaned. He slid his finger back inside her and soon she was riding his hand.

Poppy was delirious with pleasure. She sobbed his name and heat swelled inside her.

"Time for my taste now." His hand withdrew.

No. She made a sound of protest.

The beast was smiling. "I'll take care of you, my sweet anata."

He lifted and spun her. Poppy found herself bent over the curved edge of the tub.

"Is this place designed for debauchery?" she panted.

His hand ran down her back. "I've never brought anyone here."

Her chest hitched and she looked back at him. His rugged face was stark with desire. Need burned in his eyes.

"No one?" she asked.

"No one."

His hand shaped her ass and she tilted it a little.

She'd never been this shameless, or needy. His hand ran down the crevice of her buttocks, making her shiver, and he stroked her folds.

"Hot, wet, and juicy." His voice was thick with desire.

She heard water slosh, then felt warm breath on the backs of her thighs.

Oh, oh.

His mouth closed on her. His hands pushed her open. He licked and sucked, his tongue stabbing into her.

Poppy cried out, making incoherent noises. His finger found her clit as his skilled mouth kept working her.

"You taste better than I imagined, Poppy." He bit her thigh.

She jolted, sobbing now. Her breasts felt full, and throbbed. Heat coiled below in her belly.

She pushed back against his mouth and he growled against her.

"Come for me," he ordered. "Come for me, my sweetness."

Everything inside Poppy contracted. She arched her back, pure pleasure swamping her.

As waves crashed over her, she collapsed against the side of the tub. Then Brodin was moving, standing and lifting her into his arms.

He crossed to the bed, leaving a dripping path of water behind them.

Poppy's body felt heavy, lazy, and thoroughly sated.

He laid her down, pushing her thighs apart. His face looked almost feral.

She should be afraid, but instead, excitement shot through her, along with a new surge of desire.

He stroked his big hands down her thighs, his gaze on her.

God. She quivered.

This. This was what it felt like to be truly desired. To be wanted for more than her brains or ability. To be more than just looked at with faint puzzlement.

He hooked one of her thighs around his hips. His hand gripped his thick cock. The thick head rubbed against her and she bit down on her lip.

Then he thrust inside her.

Poppy moaned.

"I knew...you'd be tight." He pushed deeper. "Take me, Poppy."

Her body stretched around the hard length of him. She gripped his biceps and met his gaze.

"*Brodin.*"

"That's right. Filling you up." He started thrusting inside her, a hard, steady rhythm. "Perfect."

She moaned, her inner muscles clenching on him. *Oh, God.* Pleasure ignited like an inferno.

The look on his handsome, rugged face... His big body surged into her, his teeth gritted. She writhed, desperate to drive him as wild as she felt.

The slide of his cock sent a lightning jolt of pleasure through her body. Pleasure built until she couldn't contain it anymore. She turned her head and sank her teeth into his bicep. Her orgasm ripped through her.

His growl was low and wild. His next thrust was hard and dominant, and then his big body shuddered as his own climax hit.

They held each other, as the waves of pleasure washed over them.

CHAPTER THIRTEEN

In the early morning light, Brodin watched Poppy sleeping, filled with a sense of contentment he hadn't felt in a long time.

Leading a planet of shapeshifters with wild hearts and often volatile emotions was enormous work. He loved his people, but at times he needed a break.

Add in Zavir, and Brodin hadn't truly relaxed in a long time.

He ran his fingers over Poppy's belly. Her skin was so smooth. He liked her right here—naked, sated from him making her come, sprawled in his bed in his private lair.

His lips quirked. Yes, he was very possessive. He was growing more and more possessive of his woman from Earth.

She stirred. She opened her eyes and smiled at him.

Yeah, he liked that. He cupped her breast, and toyed with her nipple.

She gasped. "You can't want me again. Not after last night."

"You're wrong. I want you all the time." He'd used her a lot. She'd taken him—fast and hard, slow and thorough. Whatever he'd wanted, demanded of her, his sweet, sexy Poppy had given it to him.

His hand drifted down her body, and dipped between her legs.

She made a small sound.

"Sore?" He eased a finger inside her.

"A little. It's not too bad." Her hips lifted, and she bit her bottom lip.

She was already growing wet for him. She moaned.

"I want to fuck you in the traditional Damari way." The way couples and mates did.

Her eyes went wide. "How?"

"In the forest." He smiled, his gut growing hot. "After I hunt you and catch you." He thrust two fingers inside her.

"Brodin." His name ended on a moan.

He withdrew. "I'll give you a head start."

Her eyes were wide, pupils dilated, and she was breathing fast. "You want me to run outside? Naked?"

His pretty little wolf was turned on.

He nipped her lip. "Yes. There's no one around. This is my own private stretch of forest, and I don't sense any of my people close by." He lowered his head and nipped the side of her breasts, then her belly. She moaned, her hand sliding into his hair. "And it's safe. Like the safe zone, it's protected by sensors and patrols."

He bit her on the thigh.

"Okay," she said breathlessly.

His pulse spiked. He sat back. "Then run. And be ready when I catch you."

She slid off the bed, her breasts rising and falling. She was so petite, slender, and perfectly formed. He could hardly believe she could take him.

"Poppy," he growled.

She blinked, dragging her gaze off his naked body. Then she whirled and ran. She darted down the stairs, and was gone.

Brodin's blood heated, pumping thickly. He'd played with his lovers before, but he'd never hunted a woman down to claim her.

His hands flexed on the sheets, his cock hard and throbbing again. He wrapped a hand around his cock and pumped it a few times. Just the thought of running Poppy down had him on edge.

With a growl, he rose.

It was time to claim his woman.

He took the stairs two and at time, then ran into the forest.

The birds were chirping, there were rustling sounds in the undergrowth. He breathed deeply and scented Poppy—and the spice of her excited arousal.

He ran, moving fluidly. He heard animals darting away. They knew a predator was close.

But they were not his prey. He reached a clearing where her scent was stronger.

He moved to a tree and spotted claw marks. He looked up, then rammed his claws into the bark and climbed.

A strand of golden hair was caught on some leaves.

He smiled. His clever wolf. She'd slowed him down with this little trick.

He leaped off the branch and landed with a bend of his knees. He took off running again.

Poppy was smart. Ahead, she'd passed through a small creek and dispersed her scent. It took a few minutes to pick it up again.

His wolf preened. He loved to hunt challenging prey, and he was happy that his woman was so clever.

Her scent got stronger. He was close.

He heard her light footsteps. She was moving with stealth and speed, but not to the level of a trained cleaver.

Brodin cut through the trees and caught a glimpse of creamy skin and golden hair.

He smiled, desire an inferno in his gut.

She paused, looking around. So beautiful in the early-morning light. Like a nature sprite from the forest stories his mother used to tell him as a child.

He crept closer and pounced.

He took her to the ground.

"Oh, God." She wiggled and managed to get free.

She leaped up, but with a growl, Brodin chased her. A primitive smile touched his lips.

Her hair was tousled around her face, her cheeks flushed. She circled the tree, laughing, then darted off again.

He grabbed her, and she squealed and twisted.

He took her to the ground on her belly, his gaze on that sweet ass. He let his fingers explore her slick wetness.

"*Brodin.*" She pushed back against him.

Gorr, she was so tight and hot.

With his other hand, he circled his aching cock. It was so hard for her.

He covered her, notched the head of his cock between her legs, and then buried himself inside her.

His groan mingled with her shocked cry. Her inner muscles closed on his cock like a fist. He moved slowly, giving her time to get used to him.

"Move faster," she moaned.

He pulled back and yanked her hips up, then slammed back inside her.

The sound she made, the musky scent of her arousal, they all drove him crazy.

"Brodin, fuck me!"

He moved faster, harder, giving into the wild urges inside him. He needed to mark, claim, take.

"*Poppy*." He covered her and bit her shoulder.

She bucked, coming hard. Her body stiffened and shook. Her inner muscles clenched on his cock, and her scream echoed through the trees.

His own violent release slammed into him. He thrust deep and arched his back. He threw his head back and howled.

When he could think again, he was breathing hard. *Gorr*. He pulled out of her. She whimpered.

He scooped her up and looked into her wide, blue eyes, and face flushed with pleasure.

"Did I hurt you?" he growled.

She smiled. "Absolutely not."

"I'm not finished with you, yet," he said, in a gritty voice.

"Good. I'm not done with you yet, either."

She wrapped her arms around him, and he carried her back to his lair.

LATER THAT DAY, Poppy munched on a piece of guara. The fruit was crunchy on the outside, with a gooey center. *Mmm.* It tasted so good.

She'd burned a heck of a lot of calories in the last twenty-four hours. She could eat a truckload of these. She glanced at Brodin walking beside her.

Instant heat curled low in her belly. *God.* She'd become insatiable. She was sore in quite a few places.

She felt a flush of heat.

Screw it. She was not going to be embarrassed that a big, wild, hot, alien king had given her loads of off-the-charts orgasms. That he'd wanted her—sensible, smart Poppy Ellison—beyond reason thrilled her.

She'd been wild, sexy Poppy Ellison.

She smiled.

Then she remembered where they were headed, and sobered. The infirmary appeared ahead. They were going to talk to Fillian.

"Okay?" Brodin asked.

She finished the last bite of the fruit and nodded. "I'm great. Actually, I feel a little guilty to feel this good, when the teenagers are still missing. When people are still hurt."

He pulled her close and kissed her. She gripped his powerful biceps and drank him in.

"How can I want you again?" she whispered.

He shot her a wolfish grin.

She smiled and shook her head. "I've never wanted anyone like this before."

He fingered her hair. "Me neither."

She stilled. "You must have tall, gorgeous, Damari women throwing themselves at you all the time."

"Sometimes."

She smacked his arm.

He rubbed his nose against hers. "But I've never wanted any of them the way I want you. It seems I have a liking for small, blonde, smart women from Earth."

Pleasure filled her.

He took her hand and tugged her inside.

Cassanra appeared. She studied them both, then her gaze dropped to their joined hands. A smile broke out on the healer's face.

"You both look rested."

"How's Fillian?" Brodin said, smoothly ignoring the woman's teasing tone.

"He's doing much better. We'll release him today."

They walked into the room. Fillian was sitting in an armchair, not in the bed, this time. He looked much better. Annora sat beside him.

"Sire. Poppy." The man started to rise.

"Don't get up, Fillian," Brodin said. "You look much better."

"I feel much better." He waved at the synth maps on the low table in front of him. "Annora's been grilling me."

"Gently jogging your memory," the First Claw said.

The man's face twisted with frustration. "My memories really are a jumble. I wish they were clearer."

"Do you remember anything new?" Brodin asked.

The man shook his head. "Nothing of value. I know Candela and her people took me into the forest to run more experiments. I managed to get free."

"I think he was held somewhere in the Celsa Forest," Annora said.

Brodin grunted.

"That doesn't help?" Poppy asked.

Brodin stabbed at the map. "The Celsa Forest is huge. It's covered in dense vegetation, and dotted with lakes."

Poppy eyed the map.

"You didn't see any landmarks?" Annora asked Fillian.

"I remember the ceiling glowed blue." He threw his hands up. "I have no idea if that was real or not."

"What about scents?" Poppy said. "I'm learning that you Damari are all about scents." She glanced at Brodin, and they shared a private smile.

"Zhylaw chemicals." Fillian's brow furrowed. "Cats."

"Cats?" Brodin said.

"I remember a feline scent."

"Maybe creatures they're experimenting on?" Annora suggested.

"What about before that? Or after they let you out?" Poppy asked.

"The forest. Lix trees. *Wait.*" His eyes widened. "I smelled allium."

Brodin and Annora straightened.

"What's that?" Poppy asked.

"An algae that grows on the shore of a lake in the Celsa Forest," Annora answered. "It has a particular smell."

"It smells like overripe fruit," Brodin said. "It's an algae that only grows at that particular lake." He touched a large body of water on the map. "Lake Hollae."

Poppy sucked in a breath. "Candela must be close to there, somewhere."

Annora rose. "I'll organize a flyer."

"Well done, Fillian," Brodin said.

POPPY STEPPED out onto the large, semi-circular landing platform. The wind whipped at her hair as she looked down at Accalia below.

She had a bird's-eye view. She saw the market, noted the twisting pathways through the trees. Farther up the valley, she saw Brodin's cabin.

Right in front of her was a Damari flyer.

It was nothing like the sleek, little ship she and Mal had been testing for Nynatech. This flyer was built solid, from a brown metal. It had two long wings which were currently folded straight up, spearing toward the sky. They would unfold once they were airborne.

Ahead, Annora and several cleavers were already boarding. Brodin took her hand and tugged her forward.

Inside, she could see it was built as a workhorse, not for luxury. The seats were large, to fit Damari bodies, and were arranged in neat rows.

She sat beside Brodin, close to a window. At the front, in the boxy cockpit, two pilots sat at a long console.

"Prepare for flying," one pilot called back.

As they lifted off, Brodin touched a hand to her knee. "Okay?"

She nodded. "I like flying."

"You were in a bad crash."

"True, but I don't remember much of it." She looked out the window and saw the flyer's wings descend. As they flew away from the city, the wings flapped gently. Down below was a green sweep of stunning, dense forest. The trees were dark green, with pops of red here and there.

"It's not far," Brodin said.

Soon, the pilot called back. "We're coming up on Lake Hollae. We'll do a grid search over it."

"Run the scans," Brodin ordered.

Poppy spotted the glitter of the pretty lake below. The water was a brilliant blue-green. "Oh, it's gorgeous."

Brodin squeezed her hand. "I'll bring you here sometime. There's a private beach at one end that's good for swimming."

Her heart lurched. He was talking like she'd stay.

Did he want her to stay? Yes, they'd spent a frenzied night together, and were definitely compatible in bed. But that didn't translate into forever.

She kept her gaze on the lake. The few men she'd dated, including asshole Andrew, had lost interest in her eventually. Could she really hold the interest of this wild, larger-than-life man? He was an emperor, for Pete's sake.

"See anything?" Annora asked from the seat in front of them, voice tense.

"Nothing yet," Brodin said.

All Poppy could see was lake and forest. There were no signs of vehicles, buildings, or tracks.

Damn.

"Let's check on the scans." Annora rose and headed for the cockpit.

Brodin and Poppy followed.

"Do the scans show anything, Gerrant?" he asked.

The head pilot shook his head. He was young, with a clean-cut face and deep-green eyes. "Nothing that pinpoints the location, sire." The man frowned. "There are a few strange energy spikes, but we can't pinpoint an exact location."

A projection speared up like a heads-up display. It showed a graph. Poppy instantly noted the energy detection spikes. Something close by was pumping off some energy.

"Do you have more detailed scanning equipment?" she asked. "This has to be Candela. She's here, somewhere."

Brodin shook his head, frowning as he stared out the cockpit window.

"We're wolves," Annora said. "We depend on sight, sound, and scent. We can't track energy."

"But we know someone who's more attuned to energy then us," Brodin said.

Annora snapped her fingers. "The Zhaltons."

Of course. Poppy looked at the lake and forest beyond. Brodin's brother Rhain could wield energy.

And so now could Mal. The thought still shocked Poppy, but since she could grow claws, hear heartbeats, and calm wolves, she guessed she shouldn't be so surprised.

"Gerrant, get us back to Accalia. I need to call my brother. We can get some Zhaltons here to help track down Candela." Brodin's tone was dark and menacing.

Poppy took his hand, and saw him let out a breath.

"Hold on, Nayla," Annora whispered.

They had to find the kids.

CHAPTER FOURTEEN

Brodin waited on the landing pad, high above the city. Poppy and Annora stood with him.

On the landing pads below, several Damari flyers took off, soaring into the sky like giant birds. Others sat parked on the platforms, waiting to travel to other parts of Damar.

The platform he stood on was empty. Above, he saw a Zhalton shuttle appear in the sky.

He'd called Rhain several hours ago. After the attacks and deaths on Zhalto, Rhain couldn't immediately leave his planet. His people needed his visible presence, but he'd promised to send Brodin his best man.

The Zhalton shuttle flew closer. It was made from shiny, silver craxma metal, and was a much sleeker design. The engine at the back of it crackled with blue energy.

Brodin saw Poppy straighten, her gaze taking in every part of the approaching ship. He smiled. His little scientist just couldn't help herself.

The shuttle landed smoothly on the platform, a rush of warm air hitting Brodin and the women. A moment later, the side door opened.

A big man emerged, a sword sheathed at his hip.

He was very tall, very broad, and very muscular. His short, brown hair topped a masculine face, with a strong jaw, and brilliant blue eyes.

Annora groaned. "Any Zhalton but this one."

Brodin flicked a glance at her. He had noted some animosity between his First Claw and Rhain's second-in-command. "Rhain's captain of the guard is a skilled fighter."

Annora snorted. "He's rigid, unbending, and thinks he has all the answers."

"Sounds a little like you," Poppy murmured.

Annora's face soured. "Don't make me change my mind about liking you."

"Would you prefer it if I lied to you?"

The First Claw sniffed. "Be quiet."

The man stopped in front of Brodin and bowed his head. They were eye to eye. "Emperor Sarkany."

"It's Brodin. Thanks for coming, Thadd."

The man gave a brisk nod. "Zavir and his forces must be stopped." There was a dark undertone to his voice. "I'm happy to help." His gaze flicked to Annora. "First Claw."

"Captain," Annora clipped out.

Well, Brodin was surprised that the air around them didn't frost over. "And you haven't officially met Poppy, Thadd. This is Dr. Poppy Ellison."

A faint smile appeared on the captain's face. "Mal is

very happy you're doing well, Poppy. I'm Captain Thadd Naveri, captain of the guard for Overlord Sarkany."

Poppy held out her hand. "It's nice to meet you, Thadd."

"Mal's showed me how to give a proper Earth handshake." He shook her hand before looking back at Brodin. "So, where do we start?"

"We'll meet with my cleavers, brief you, and make a plan."

They headed to the lodge where the cleavers were waiting.

"Are you able to access energy from Damar's magnetic field?" Poppy asked Thadd.

"A little. It's not as strong as on Zhalto, but I can still use some energy here."

They entered the main meeting room. Most of the cleavers lounged in chairs around the table. Tolf was pacing at the back.

A map of the forest and lake was projected up on the wall.

"Cleavers," Brodin said. "Captain Thadd Naveri of Zhalto."

Thadd nodded at the men and women.

Annora stepped forward. "We've pinpointed Candela to this area, based on our rescued hunter's intel." She turned. "We've done flyovers, and we're detecting energy spikes that we think are coming from Candela's base, but we can't pinpoint an exact location."

Thadd studied the map and nodded. "It would be better if I'm on the ground."

"You can't go alone," Brodin said. "You don't know the area, and Candela is snatching lone hunters."

"If the team is too large, we'll be detected," Thadd said. "Stealth would be better."

Annora straightened, her spine ramrod straight. "I'll take him. I'll have a flyer drop us close. We can run search patterns." She gave Thadd a look. "If you can keep up."

A muscle ticked in Thadd's strong jaw. "I can keep up."

Brodin nodded. "All right, Annora and Thadd will carry out the ground search." He thumped his fist on the table. "And we need to do something to draw Candela's attention and keep her from detecting you two. There's also a chance that she might give away her base location, as well."

Tolf nodded. "We could take out a group. Make a ruckus."

Poppy stepped forward. "Use me."

Brodin's chest contracted. "No."

"Brodin, she wants me. She knows I can help nullify the effect of her toxin. Use me as bait, but have your cleavers close. If she's busy chasing me, it gives Annora and Thadd a better chance to track the energy signatures."

Brodin growled, and everyone in the room tensed.

Except Poppy.

She stepped up to him and rolled her eyes. "Yes, yes, you're very scary."

Someone nearby nervously cleared their throat.

Brodin couldn't think through his rage. His hands

curled. She wanted to put herself in danger. He couldn't let Candela get her hands on Poppy.

Annora moved up beside Poppy. "She makes a good point, Brodin."

"No," he growled.

"Think it through," his First Claw said. "You'll be with her. She'll be with a team of your best cleavers."

Poppy pressed her hands to his chest. "I want to help. I need to help bring those kids home."

Air shuddered out of him. "*Gorr.*" He reached around her, grabbed a mug off the table, and threw it at the wall.

No one even blinked.

She smiled. "I knew you'd see reason."

He yanked her up on her toes and kissed her. He didn't care about the room full of people. He kissed her until she gasped, her face dazed.

He set her down. Around them, his people grinned, purposely looking at the projected map.

"All right, Annora and Thadd, get the supplies you need. Everyone else, prepare. We'll meet at the flyer platforms."

Back at his cabin, Brodin led Poppy up to his bedroom.

"I have something for you."

She raised a brow.

He waved a hand at the bed and saw her suck in a breath.

It was leather armor, perfectly matched to her size. He'd asked an artisan to make it for her. It had similar designs to his own etched into it.

"Brodin—"

"I want you protected, Poppy. I need you protected."

"We're going to stop Candela." Poppy went up on her toes and kissed him. "It's all going to be okay."

Brodin nodded, but he knew things didn't always work out the way you planned.

He went to change into his own armor. He strapped his axe to his back, and secured his hair at the base of his neck. He was in the living room, tying on his sturdy boots, when Poppy came down the stairs.

He stared at her.

She eyed him. "God, you're hot."

And she looked like a Damari. The leather molded to her body, like his hands did when he had her naked. She'd left her blonde hair loose and her face was composed, focused.

He pulled her close and kissed her. "This is for you." He held out a dagger.

"Oh, it's beautiful." She stroked the hilt that was set with blue jewels.

"It's a damar stone. Mined in the mountains of Yarfell." He didn't tell her that it was rare and priceless.

"Thank you."

He helped her strap the dagger to her thigh.

"I don't want you to do this," he said.

"I know." She patted his cheek. "A part of me doesn't want to either, but those teenagers must be so scared."

He cupped her cheek. "*Gorr*, I wish you weren't so brave."

She smiled. "I've never been called brave before."

He held her hand as they headed to the landing pads.

The flyer was ready, the engines droning. The cleavers were already on board, along with Annora and Thadd.

As soon as Brodin gave the order, they lifted off.

Brodin watched Accalia disappear behind them. They sailed over the trees and the glint of the lake shone in the distance.

He dragged in a deep breath.

Candela would not get her poisonous hands on Poppy. He'd do whatever he had to do to keep her safe.

Soon, the flyer slowed and moved into a hover.

"We're at the drop off point for the First Claw," the pilot called out.

Brodin opened the side door. Annora and Thadd stepped up beside him.

"Good hunting," Brodin said.

"See you soon." Without warning, Annora leaped out of the flyer. It was a long drop, but nothing a Damari couldn't handle.

She plummeted down to the small clearing below.

With a nod, Thadd leaped out after her. Brodin felt a pulse of energy fill the air, as the Zhalton used energy to slow his fall.

He landed beside Annora in a crouch.

As the flyer wheeled away, Brodin prayed that the pair tracked down Candela's base.

THEIR SMALL GROUP jogged through the forest. It had rained recently, and the ground was wet and muddy. Poppy leaped over a puddle.

Around her, the cleavers melted into the trees. She couldn't sense them any longer, but Brodin stayed with her.

"Tolf is going to set off some flares," he said. "Let Candela know we're here."

She nodded, fighting her nerves. She hoped that Thadd and Annora were okay.

"You don't have to do this," Brodin said.

She met his gaze and saw the sheen of gold roll over the blue. "Yes, I do."

He released a ragged breath. Suddenly, there was a sharp whistle and they both looked up. She saw something shoot into the sky.

A flare erupted in sparks of red. Then another one.

"Come on." Brodin pushed the bushes aside.

They heard shouts in the distance. They both froze. Brodin cocked his head, listening.

"What's going on?" she whispered.

"I'm not sure."

They kept moving. They reached a huge tree, with a massive trunk that was enormous. Monkey-like creatures sat in the branches, with huge eyes that made them look cute. The branches spread out wide, and long narrow leaves dripped downward.

Suddenly, the monkeys froze, then disappeared, moving higher up in the tree.

Poppy's heart thumped. They were scared of something. A long howl made the hairs on the back of her neck rise.

Then, a pained scream cut through the trees.

Brodin tensed. "Someone's hurt." He broke into a run.

Poppy followed. Soon, she was sweating and breathing hard. Ahead, she heard the sound of fighting.

An astringent scent made her wrinkle her nose. It smelled like strong chemicals.

They burst out of the trees.

She noted the lake in the background, just as a large, cat-like creature bounded across the clearing and pounced on a cleaver. It took the woman to the ground.

More of the beasts appeared. They looked like large jaguars. Most of them were brown, with darker, mottled patches. They had large heads with huge jaws, and a long tail tipped with spikes.

Oh. *God*.

All around, the cleavers—some in wolf form, some part shifted—were fighting the cats.

"Poppy, stay hidden," Brodin growled.

"I will. Go."

He met her gaze for a searing second, then he pulled his huge axe from over his shoulder.

With a roar, he charged into the fight.

His deadly axe sliced through the air, cutting into a cat clawing at one of his cleavers. Black blood sprayed. The cleaver rolled, and Brodin pulled her up.

Another cleaver used a short sword, hacking into one of the cats. Poppy watched as the animal twisted and hissed. It swiped at the cleaver with massive claws.

That claw looked familiar. She sucked in a breath. This was the creature that had menaced her and those two teens in the forest.

Nearby, another wolf and cat were locked in combat. Then, a low snarl behind her made her freeze.

Oh, shit.

She gripped her dagger, and pulled it slowly from the sheath on her thigh. She turned her head.

A huge, black cat was slinking out of the shadows under the trees. Its fur was mottled.

Oh, hell, it was massive.

Poppy swallowed. Its head was level with her chest and it had a powerful body, but it reeked of decay. Several metallic implants were dotted along its body, and each paw was tipped with ridiculously long claws.

Nice kitty. Poppy backed up slowly.

She saw its muscles tense, readying to jump.

She sucked in a breath. The beast leaped, and she dropped to the ground and crawled under it.

Jumping up, she ran for the nearest tree. Her claws slid out, and she leaped at the trunk, her claws digging into the bark. She climbed.

The Zhylaw cat jumped after her. She felt claws snag on her boot. Poppy kicked the cat in the face, and it dropped to the ground with a snarl.

Rising, she walked along a thick branch. All around, the fight raged. She watched one cleaver dump a cat in the lake. Brodin's lethal axe was hacking into others.

An enraged hiss made her look down...

Just as the cat hunting her leaped up at her branch.

Heart in her throat, she dodged the claws and kicked it.

The tips of two claws slashed her cheek, her skin stinging hotly.

The cat leaped back down to the ground, but Poppy lost her balance.

She teetered on the branch.

Shit, shit, shit.

She threw her arms out, but not even her new Damari strength and agility could help her. She fell backward.

Poppy had no time to think. She hit the ground on her back, the wind knocked out of her. Her bones rattled.

She groaned, trying to pull in air.

Move, Poppy, move.

She pushed to her feet, her body one massive ache. She spotted the cat stalking toward her, its green eyes glowing.

Another one joined it.

Shit.

Poppy turned, scrambled up, and ran.

She crashed through the trees, pushing for more speed. She dodged around a thick trunk and straight through some low bushes. Thorns pulled and scratched at her leather armor.

A cat leaped in from her right, and she swiveled and ran between two larger trees.

The second beast snarled from the left, and she dodged it. For some reason, they weren't attacking her.

She leaped over a rotting stump covered with moss.

That's when it hit her. They were *herding* her.

She couldn't hear sounds of fighting anymore, dammit.

Suddenly, a person stepped into Poppy's path.

She skidded to a halt.

Candela smiled, her creepy, black-and-red hair waving around her thin face like a breeze was blowing.

Except there was no breeze.

"Hello, there." The warlord held up her claw-tipped gloves. "I've been looking for you."

Poppy backed up a step, but a cat hissed, freezing her in her tracks. Both animals were behind her.

"You seem to have the power to derail all my carefully laid plans," Candela said.

Poppy lifted her chin. "Good. You're scum. You have talents, but you use them for evil. To hurt and torture."

Candela rolled her eyes. "Who says everything has to be good? I like to kill. I'm good at it, and Zavir appreciates my skill. I don't need your self-righteous ramblings about doing good for everyone."

Clearly, the bitch was rotten to the core.

And there was no way Poppy was going anywhere with her.

Poppy's claws slid out.

Then she leaped at the warlord.

CHAPTER FIFTEEN

Brodin cut down another Zhylaw cat. He was splattered with blood and gore.

He shook his head. The blood of Zhylaw beasts always reeked, and the rank odor was stuck in his senses.

The rest of his cleavers were finishing off the last of the cats.

He glanced around the field, looking for Poppy.

His chest locked.

There was no sign of her.

He strode toward the trees and breathed deeply.

"Sire?" Gwenna said.

"Find Poppy's scent."

It was hard to sniff past the Zhylaw stench.

There.

He saw claw marks on a tree and branch. There was a muddy patch on the ground, and he spotted her footprints leading into the forest.

Followed by the prints of two cats.

"On me," he roared.

He ran as fast as he could, following the trail.

I'm coming, Poppy.

Poppy was smart. She'd find a way to stall until he got there.

The sounds of fighting ahead caught his ear. He pushed for more speed, pulling ahead of his cleavers.

He broke through the trees in time to see Poppy and Candela collide.

The warlord's poisonous hair hit Poppy's face and neck, turning Poppy's skin gray.

She ran her claws into Candela's gut.

That was his fierce woman.

Candela grunted. She wore slick, black armor that Poppy's claws didn't penetrate, but he knew she'd feel the blows.

Brodin smiled grimly and started forward. He watched Candela swipe out with her clawed glove.

Using Damari quickness, Poppy dodged.

Suddenly, one of the mutant cats leaped at Brodin with a vicious snarl.

He grabbed the animal, gripping its fur hard. It snapped its jaws and hissed. He strained to keep its fangs away from his face.

He gripped the mottled fur harder and slammed the beast into the ground.

Gritting his teeth, he held the cat and twisted. The beast's neck snapped with a crack. He shoved the body away.

Cleavers streamed in, taking on the other cat.

Candela and Poppy whirled. The warlord slashed

with her claws and Poppy jumped back, tripping over a small log.

No.

She fell on her back.

Candela smiled.

Then, her arm moving so fast it was a blur, Poppy threw her dagger.

It cut into Candela's left eye. The warlord screamed and staggered back.

Poppy scrambled to her feet.

"Poppy," Brodin roared.

She ran to him.

Candela spun, clutching her injured eye, and saw him. She yanked the dagger out, blood pouring down her cheek. Her cry filled the clearing.

Then she lifted her whistle and blew.

The resulting sound was piercing, and Brodin winced. He heard his cleavers curse.

Two new cats bounded out of the forest toward the warlord.

As they got close, Candela sank a hand into the fur of one and swung onto the animal's back. The cats sprinted into the trees.

Poppy reached him and he clasped her to him.

"Are you all right?" he asked.

She nodded, clutching him tightly. "I'm fine."

He pulled her close and pressed his face to her hair. He'd been terrified, but she was alive, and unhurt. He let out a shuddering breath.

"Sire, should we give chase?" a cleaver asked.

Brodin scanned his pack. A few were bleeding. All of them looked battered and weary. He shook his head.

"Let's return to the meeting point. We'll deal with everyone's wounds, recuperate, and wait for Annora and the captain."

Brodin lifted Poppy off her feet.

"Brodin, I can walk."

He ignored her.

She rolled her eyes, but didn't say anything else, just slid her arm along his shoulders.

They jogged through the trees to the prearranged meeting point. If Annora and Thadd found anything, they would meet them here.

Brodin stopped at a particularly huge tree. It had an absolutely massive trunk, wider than a vehicle.

He set Poppy down and pressed his palms to the bark.

A moment later, there was a click and a small doorway opened in the trunk. The inside of the trunk had been hollowed out, and a ladder stood inside the space.

Poppy gasped.

"Tolf, go first," Brodin ordered.

The tracker disappeared up the ladder.

"Gwenna and Jennete, you're on sentry duty." They were two of the uninjured cleavers. With nods, they melted into the forest.

"Up you go," he told Poppy.

She gripped the ladder and climbed. Brodin helped the injured cleavers up, and closed the door to the hideout behind him.

At the top of the ladder was a huge platform, ringed

with a wooden railing, and hidden in the dense foliage of the tree.

Their medic was already treating the injured.

Poppy wandered to the railing, peering through the branches. "What is this place?"

He pulled her against him, grateful that she was okay.

"It's a tracker hideout. They can use it for shelter, or to monitor the forest and animals. We have them dotted throughout the forest."

She nodded.

He stroked her face, his fingers gently brushing the gray patches where the poison had killed her skin.

"It doesn't hurt," she said quietly.

"Another thing for Candela to pay for."

"Let's just be thankful Candela's hair isn't dipped with the Damari poison she's cooking up." Poppy gripped his wrist and stroked. "I gave her a few bruises."

Brodin smiled. "My bloodthirsty woman." He lowered his head and kissed her.

He made the medic check Poppy over. The man put some poultice on the poison spots on her face. Brodin could see they weren't too bad, and were already healing.

When the medic assessed her ribs, Poppy winced.

"Um, I fell out of a tree."

Brodin frowned.

The medic checked her more thoroughly. "Nothing's broken, luckily. You're just bruised."

Finally, they all settled in on the platform, eating jerky rations and drinking water.

"What now?" Poppy asked.

"We wait for Annora and Thadd."

"God, I hope they find whatever rock Candela is hiding under."

With that, they rested. The quiet of the forest was punctuated by the rustling of leaves in the gentle breeze, the chirp of birds, and the hum of insects. Some of the cleavers dozed, used to catching quick naps when they could.

Suddenly, the trap door opened, and one of the sentries appeared.

"Sire, I spotted the First Claw and Captain Naveri. They are headed this way and moving fast."

Brodin rose.

Moments later, Annora and Thadd climbed onto the platform.

"You're both okay?" Brodin asked.

Annora nodded. She scanned the injured. "What happened?"

"Candela. She had a pack of Zhylaw cats."

Annora's mouth flattened. "We found the base."

Brodin looked at Thadd.

The man nodded. "I could easily track the energy signatures."

"Where?"

Annora straightened. "In the lake."

Poppy blinked. *What?*

Brodin frowned. "What do you mean, in the lake?"

"She's hiding her base under the water," Thadd said.

Brodin sucked in a sharp breath. "It makes sense. The water must muffle sound and drown out any scents."

"She's virtually undetectable to Damari senses," Annora added.

A grim smile touched Brodin's lips. "But not anymore. Candela's reign of terror ends now."

POPPY STOOD at the lake's edge, staring at the pretty, blue water.

Some cleavers were too injured to swim and would wait for them here.

She turned the small device in her palm over. It looked a little like a harmonica. The others held them, as well.

Brodin explained that it was a re-breathing unit that would allow her to breathe under the water. She really wanted to pull it apart and see how it worked. Maybe she'd be able to, later.

Brodin, Annora, and Thadd were talking quietly together, their expressions tense.

The plan was to swim down and do some recon on Candela's base.

How the hell had she hidden it in the middle of the lake? Poppy looked back at the lake. They were close to ending this, she could feel it.

The kids could be there. They were so close. She saw how edgy Annora was. The woman wanted her sister back safely.

The First Claw looked up and traded a glare with Thadd.

And it seemed the captain rubbed the First Claw the wrong way.

"All right." Brodin faced the group. "We swim down

and stay together. It will get dark in the water as we descend. We find Candela's base and gather intel. If we spot the young ones, and we can free them safely, we will. If not, we regroup and get reinforcements."

Annora shifted impatiently.

"Let's go." Brodin put the breathing unit in his mouth.

Poppy followed suit. He reached out to adjust hers a little, and stroked her jaw.

Then, they waded into the jewel-blue water.

Poppy sucked in a breath. It was colder than she'd anticipated. The water hit her knees, thighs, waist.

She watched Annora dive under, then Thadd, the other cleavers, and Brodin.

She took another breath, steeled herself, and dived.

After the first shock of cold passed, she realized it wasn't too bad. She saw Brodin ahead, kicking strongly.

Poppy frowned. The water was a pretty color, but a little murky. As they descended, it got darker.

Suddenly, Brodin was beside her, taking her hand. His kicks were powerful enough to tow her deeper.

She spotted Annora not far ahead, swimming like a seal. Thadd's kicks were strong and even. The other cleavers were in the shadows, close by.

The last of the light petered out, and that's when Poppy noted a faint, blue glow from below.

Knots formed in her belly, and her pulse tripped. The light was coming from the depths of the lake.

There was definitely something down there.

They swam on. Some sleek, spotted fish swam past them, curious and quick. But as she looked straight down, she saw a large shape slowly emerge from the darkness.

Brodin's fingers squeezed on hers.

It was a spaceship.

Poppy could see the bulk of it, but it was dominated by a large, blue dome that was clouded over and glowed blue.

Annora pointed. They swam closer, avoiding getting too close to the dome.

They moved along the side of the vessel. It was made of a dark-bronze colored metal.

They stopped, with their backs pressed to the side. Ahead, there was a large opening in the ship. As they watched, two of the cat creatures swam down from above and into the long, narrow opening.

Apparently Zhylaw cats didn't mind the water, or whatever the Zhylaw did to them overrode any natural aversion.

Brodin squeezed her hand, and waved to the others. They floated closer.

Annora and Thadd swam in through the opening first.

Poppy waited, her heart hammering in her ears.

Then, Annora reappeared and waved them in.

They swam through the opening. The dark metal formed a rectangular tunnel. Annora reached a wall, and swam straight up.

They broke the surface of the water and came out in a pool in the middle of a large chamber.

It was like a moon pool on diving and marine vessels on Earth, that provided easy access to the water. The chamber had metal walls, with some equipment stored on racks. She suspected it was the Zhylaw's diving gear.

There was no sign of the cats. Thadd crouched at the edge of the pool and pulled Poppy out. Brodin and the others climbed up behind her.

They were inside Candela's ship.

"The cats went that way." Annora pointed to a door. Wet puddles rested on the floor. "I can scent them."

"Move silently," Brodin murmured. "Any trouble, we head back here and swim out."

Poppy followed him. The corridor they entered was large and sparse. There were some glowing controls on the wall, but not much else.

Howls echoed through the ship. The Damari all froze.

"Was that a Damari?" Poppy whispered.

"I can't tell," Brodin responded.

They followed the sound, and a hum of energy filled the air. Poppy's heart thudded in her chest.

At the end of the tunnel lay a large doorway. They all stayed close to the wall as they jogged toward it.

When they reached the doorway, Poppy heard Annora suck in a sharp breath.

The doorway led into a huge room under the dome.

The blue dome soared above, but it was the strange machine in the center of the space that caught Poppy's attention.

What the hell was that?

It looked like several translucent boxes, cobbled together. The structure glowed, pulsing with internal light.

Several slender scientists in black uniforms were working on the machine, monitoring it.

"Brodin, look," Tolf murmured.

The cleaver was looking to the left and Poppy followed his gaze. She heard Brodin's low growl.

Five young Damari, caught between youth and adulthood, hung in what looked like columns of blue light.

"Stasis fields." Annora's voice was tight. She was looking at the pretty, young brunette at the end.

Her sister looked like a softer, younger version of Annora.

The kids weren't moving. Their chins were tipped to their chests and they were floating in the light.

There was no way to tell if they were hurt.

"Annora, and the rest of you, free the young ones," Brodin ordered. "Poppy, Thadd, and I will take a close look at the machine."

"Where's Candela?" Thadd growled.

"I don't see her," Brodin replied, "but stay alert. She's here somewhere."

Poppy and Brodin crept forward. Thadd was one step behind them. They skirted boxes, crates, empty cages. There were several bunks—all empty—but the horrible manacles hanging off each of them warned what they were used for.

Poppy swallowed.

"Energy levels off the machine are unbelievably high," Thadd said.

"Let's ask our Zhylaw friends some questions," Brodin said darkly.

They picked up speed. The scientists didn't hear them coming.

Brodin grabbed a male Zhylaw and spun him around. The man's eyes bugged out of his head at the sight of them, and he spluttered.

Brodin gripped the man's neck and lifted him off his feet. He slammed him against the side of the machine.

Thadd grabbed two scientists and knocked their heads together. He released them and they dropped to the floor.

A female opened her mouth and Poppy held her claws to the woman's neck. "Quiet."

The woman froze.

Brodin glared at the male, until the man's gaze dropped to the floor.

"You'll answer my questions, or I'll gut you and leave you bleeding. Understand?"

The man nodded rapidly.

"What does this machine do?"

The Zhylaw swallowed and stayed silent. Brodin shook him.

"I-I it's a disperser. When the ship is airborne, it will pump poison into the planet's atmosphere."

Poppy went still. "What poison?"

The man swallowed rapidly.

"What poison?" Brodin growled.

"The poison Candela developed that drives the Damari wild," the man said in a rush.

Poppy's insides froze. *Oh, no.*

CHAPTER SIXTEEN

Brodin tried to control the molten rage inside him. Candela wanted to drive every single one of his people—man, woman, and child—mad. She wanted them to kill each other, blindly murder their own loved ones.

And this worm was helping her.

His claws tightened. The scientist whimpered.

"How do you deactivate it?" Poppy asked.

"I don't know—"

Brodin shook the man.

"I don't, I swear. All I know is that there is a panel at the very top that Candela doesn't let anyone near."

"Brodin!" Thadd yelled.

Snarls and hisses filled the dome.

Brodin turned his head, and spotted several Zhylaw cats entering the room.

The one in the lead was huge, with pure-black fur—the alpha.

"Lock the scientists in a cage," Brodin ordered.

Thadd nodded and yanked the scientist in front of him closer.

"Brodin, I need to get to the top of the machine and take a closer look," Poppy said. "I need to find a way to deactivate and destroy it."

If anyone could do it, it was Poppy.

He tugged her close for a quick kiss. "Do it. Stay safe."

"You, too." She kissed him back. "Give me a boost?"

He gripped her waist and tossed her upward.

She flew through the air and grabbed the side of the machine, scrambling up onto one of its many ledges.

Brodin turned to face the cats.

The stench of rot and decay wafted from them. Time to put them down. His claws lengthened and his body semi-shifted. He felt his muscles and bones growing.

Across the space, he saw Annora had three of the kids out of the stasis fields, but the cats were coming. Brodin had to buy her more time.

With a roar, he sprinted toward the cats. He leaped over a crate, and a cat ran at him.

They both went airborne. Brodin slashed, catching the cat's face. Black blood sprayed.

As soon as he hit the floor, he spun and thrust his claws into its side, cutting it open. It fell, and he kicked it aside.

Two more cats were slinking close. "Come on, then." He lifted his claws.

The beasts dashed at him. He swung his claws, gouging deep. One cat let out a sharp cry.

The second beast hit Brodin's back, its claws biting deep into his armor.

He felt the sting of poison. *Gorr.* These ones had poison on their claws. He reached over his shoulder and yanked the cat off him. He threw it to the floor.

It tried to right itself, but Brodin jumped. He landed on top of it. He gripped one of its legs and crushed it with a crunch of bone.

The cat's screech was deafening.

Turning, he headed toward the cats attacking Annora's team.

He slashed until the floor was slick with black blood.

His claws stuck in the rib cage of one cat, and when another one leaped, Brodin threw out his other arm and grabbed the animal.

It hissed. He threw it with all his strength, and it crashed into the wall. He heard bones crunch. It slid down the wall and didn't get up.

He glanced at the machine and his heart stopped.

Poppy was climbing higher. *Where the gorr was she going?*

That's when he saw Candela was climbing after her.

There you are. Rage contracted to a hard point in his gut. The Zhylaw witch would not hurt his woman.

Brodin started across the space.

The alpha cat leaped into his path and snarled. Its lips lifted to show razor-sharp fangs.

Brodin scowled, raised his claws, and howled. He launched at the cat.

The cat darted to the side, fast. Impossibly fast.

As the cat leaped, Brodin jumped to meet it.

They crashed into each other. He felt the slash of claws as he rammed his into black fur.

They hit the floor and rolled.

Brodin's back smashed against a crate, and it splintered with the crunch. He released the cat and rolled onto his feet.

This one was faster and stronger than the others.

He risked a quick glance at Poppy. He saw her kicking at Candela.

Brodin growled.

He needed to help her.

Quickly, he pulled the quick-release bindings on his armor. He ripped it off, then shucked his shirt and pants. The cat snarled at him, watching him cautiously, readying to attack.

He let the change flow over him. His muscles stretched and lengthened. Fur formed.

His senses shifted to damar-wolf. His large paws slapped the floor.

The alpha cat snarled, and Brodin howled.

They sprinted at each other, and leaped.

They tore into each other, claws slashing and jaws snapping.

Brodin felt the sting of claws and poison, but he ignored it. The fight turned brutal.

He pivoted, his fangs bared, and darted in again. His jaws closed on the cat's back leg. Something snapped.

With a yelp, the cat leaped back, holding one leg off the ground. Its eyes glowed bright green.

They circled each other.

Brodin went in for the kill.

This time he closed his jaws on the .cat's neck. It twisted and struggled, but Brodin kept his tight grip on the beast. He bit down harder. Claws raked his gut, but he doggedly held on.

The cat stilled and Brodin jerked his head, tearing flesh. Blood splattered, and the alpha cat slumped.

With a shake of his head, Brodin tossed the body aside.

Then he started toward the machine and shifted back. The change flowed over him, and he straightened, his body back to that of a man. He stopped to yank on his discarded pants, but there was no time for his armor. He ran to the machine.

Candela and Poppy were facing off right at the top.

He saw Candela swipe out with her claw-tipped hands.

Poppy jumped back and lost her balance. She teetered on the edge.

No.

She windmilled her arms and caught herself.

Brodin pressed his hands to the machine and started climbing.

He had to reach Poppy.

He had to stop Candela.

POPPY GRITTED her teeth and faced Candela.

The woman had an eyepatch over the eye Poppy had injured.

Poppy needed the warlord out of the way, so she

could deactivate the machine. There was no time to look down, but she knew the fight was still raging below.

"You will die here," Candela drawled.

"How's that eye doing?" Poppy asked. "I might cut out your other one next."

The warlord's face twisted. "I'll make sure you die painfully. I'm sorry you won't get to see this savage planet tear itself apart." She flung her arm out. "These animals will get what they deserve."

"Those *animals* are a thousand times better than you." The Damari were caring and loving. They cared for their planet, the environment, their pack, and Brodin cared for her before he'd even known her.

She was in love with him.

Butterflies filled her, but she had no time to think about it.

Candela's hair waved around her face. "I'm a genius, and my success here will simply prove it."

"You're scum. And you will die here today."

Candela lunged.

Poppy was ready. She used the move that Annora had showed her.

She dropped and swiped her leg out. She knocked Candela off her feet and, with a cry, the warlord fell.

Over the edge.

Yes! Elation rocketed through Poppy, and she scrambled over to the drop-off.

But the Zhylaw woman hadn't fallen to the bottom, dammit. She was flat on her back, one level down.

She wasn't moving, but even from here, Poppy could tell she was still breathing.

Turning, Poppy climbed to the top of the machine. There were several panels set in the surface.

Using her new Damari strength, she tore the panels open.

Her belly cramped.

The inside looked like nothing she'd ever worked with on Earth.

"You're smart, Poppy, you will work it out," she muttered.

She had to.

Lives—so many lives—depended on it.

Including Brodin's.

She started pulling up bits of tech—wires, piping filled with fluid. Poppy's brow creased and she got to work.

She hummed to herself, trying not to imagine what was going on down below. She definitely needed to cut these lines.

Yanking them out, she watched the lights on the side of the machine flicker and die.

She grinned. *Yes.*

She kept yanking, and found something resembling a circuit board. The best way to deactivate the bomb would be to ruin the power supply to the machine.

She smashed the board.

More lights flickered and went out.

"No!"

Candela launched over the edge and ran at Poppy.

Shit.

Poppy jumped up. The warlord dived, grabbing at Poppy's legs, and tackled her.

They slammed onto the machine. The woman's hair whipped around, stabbing at Poppy's stomach.

She smelled something burning, and saw the poison from the woman's hair was melting Poppy's leather armor.

Crap. She bucked and tried to dislodge Candela.

Suddenly, her belly stung. *Ow.* The poison had worked through to her skin.

She reared up and punched Candela in the face. The woman howled, her nose broken, blood gushing from it.

On her hands and knees, Poppy scrambled back to the open panel and yanked more things out.

Frustratingly, nothing else turned off. The machine still hummed.

Dammit.

Candela rose, laughing. God, she was annoying.

"Oh, tone down the clichéd evil warlord, would you?" Poppy snapped.

"I told you that I'd win. My machine has several redundancies built into it. You won't be able to deactivate it."

"Watch me."

"No, I'll kill you, instead. If not for you, this horrid world would still be scrambling, dealing with a massacre, letting me perfect my machine in peace." She launched at Poppy.

They traded blows. Poppy blocked the woman's hits and got in a kick. She sliced with her claws, and several slashes opened up on Candela's suit.

The warlord hissed in pain and leaped back, her face contorting.

Poppy glared. "It's not so easy when you don't have your mutated beasts with you, or your enemy isn't strapped down to a bench, now is it?"

Candela made an enraged sound.

They crashed together again, and Poppy tripped. The warlord fell on top of her. They slid over the machine's slick surface.

Poppy punched Candela, but her hair wrapped around Poppy's arm, pulling it back.

Poison burned her skin. Poppy gritted her teeth and rammed her claws into Candela's shoulder.

With a scream, the warlord rolled off her.

Poppy was right near an open panel. She reached in and pulled out some fluid-filled sacs and a glowing crystal. She threw everything at Candela.

Then, inside, down deep, she saw blinking lights. A buried control panel of some sort.

If she could—

Candela's foot connected with Poppy's face. It wasn't that hard, but she tasted blood in her mouth. She realized then that Candela wasn't a very physical fighter. Poppy wasn't either, but since her transformation, she had more strength.

She jumped up and executed a perfect kick. Candela flew back.

Annora would be proud.

"*Enough.*" Candela rose and wiped the blood off her mouth with the back of her hand. Her eyepatch was askew.

Then she pulled a slim device off her belt.

Poppy frowned and tensed. *What the hell was that?*

Candela held it up and a stream of blue energy shot from it like a laser.

Shit. Poppy dived and rolled, trying not to get too close to the edge of the machine.

The beam cut into the metal, leaving a burned, melted incision.

Uh-oh. Not good.

Poppy leaped up and dodged again.

Candela fired again, and Poppy ducked.

She had nowhere to go, unless she jumped off the machine and risked breaking a lot of bones.

Candela's smile turned smug. "I promise this will hurt a lot."

Suddenly a huge, muscular form leaped over the edge, and slammed into Candela.

Her laser firearm flew out of her hand and sailed over the edge of the machine.

Brodin rose and Poppy's pulse went crazy.

He was bare chested and shoeless, his muscles flexing.

His hot gaze ran over Poppy, before it settled on the warlord.

The emperor of the Damari looked wild and fierce.

CHAPTER SEVENTEEN

Growling, Brodin fought back his rage.

Poppy was okay, but Candela would pay for touching her.

"Ah, the king of the filthy shapeshifters arrives." Candela's smile was ugly, her hair whipping angrily around her face. "You and your kind should be in a cage, or strapped to one of my lab tables. You can't stop me now." She kicked a foot against the machine under them. "This device will deliver my exquisite creation to your entire planet. You will die like the animals you are. Tearing, ripping, and biting."

"You bitch!" Poppy ran forward, her claws raised.

Her claws caught on Candela's fake ones. Brodin swallowed a curse.

"And·you—" the women strained against each other "—you, I'll take to my lab." Candela met Brodin's gaze over Poppy's head, and he knew this was a threat just for him. "I'll cut her open and find out what makes her tick. Her screams will fill my lab."

Brodin flexed his claws and wanted to charge.

Candela shoved Poppy, and she flew backward. Brodin lunged and caught her.

"Okay?" he asked.

She nodded. "You?"

"I will be soon."

"You can't stop my device." Candela straightened. "You're wasting your time."

"It's a lie," Poppy murmured to Brodin. "I can do it, but I have to get inside the machine." She jerked her head toward the open panel.

"All right. I'll deal with Candela, you get in there."

She nodded, her gaze locked on his. "Don't get hurt, Brodin."

Gorr, he wanted to kiss her. "Once this is over, we'll go back to my lair. I have lots more plans for you, Poppy Ellison."

She smiled. "Deal."

They turned toward Candela.

Brodin stalked toward the warlord, and the woman's single eye narrowed on him. Then it flicked briefly to Poppy, making her way toward the panel.

"Oh, no, you don't." She yanked something off her belt and threw it.

Metal rolled across the surface of the machine, slowed, then burst open.

The small device looked like a metallic spider. It skittered on its legs, then launched at Poppy.

"Poppy, look out!" Brodin roared.

She threw an arm up. The device clamped on her forearm, and she screamed.

"Poppy—" He'd taken one step when Candela raced at him. She raked him with her claws.

Brodin leaped back. Three raw scratches opened up on his chest.

Poppy was panting. She reached up with her free hand and broke the legs off the metal creature. She cried out, then tore it off her arm. It hit the ground, and she stomped on it.

"Poppy?" he called out.

She cradled her arm against her chest, her face pinched. "I'm fine. It burns, but I'm already feeling better."

He turned to Candela. *Enough.* He stepped forward.

Candela's eye widened. She threw more balls at him.

Mid-air, they also burst into spiders, and clamped on to his chest.

Ah, gorr. The pain was excruciating. The legs dug into his skin, pumping poison into him.

Like Poppy had said, it burned.

Candela laughed, and the sound was filled with delight. She clearly enjoyed other people's pain.

Brodin gritted his teeth and yanked the devices off, one by one.

Out of the corner of his eye, he saw Poppy dive into a hole in the machine.

Good. His gorgeous woman would stop it.

He looked back at Candela, and caught a look of panic in the warlord's eye.

A shot of savage satisfaction filled him. "Ah, not so sure of your device after all?"

The warlord's mouth flattened. "I'll enjoy watching

you and your whore racing around, trying to save the day."

"I'll enjoy stabbing you with my claws and watching the light fade from your eyes." He smiled. "I mean eye. My woman already took care of your other one."

"If you do that, Brodin, at least it will stop her yapping." It was Annora's voice. His First Claw pulled herself over the edge. "You hurt my sister, you *gorr*-cursed witch." Annora's claws slid free.

Thadd pulled himself up beside Annora, and yanked his sword free of its scabbard.

It lit up, glowing with gold energy.

Annora ran across the top of the machine, her long legs flying.

Candela threw up her arm and touched the band on her wrist.

A blue energy shield flared to life. Annora hit her and it sizzled. His First Claw flew backward, then caught herself in a crouch.

"Oh, this is working very nicely." Candela smiled at the shield. "It's still experimental and untested, you know."

Thadd started forward, his face grim.

"Well. A Zhalton." Candela studied him. "I heard you spent some quality time with Krastin, Captain Naveri."

A muscle ticked in Thadd's jaw. He swung his sword.

It hit Candela's energy shield and shimmered.

"How about we try this sweet little invention next?" She held up her claw glove. The center of the palm started to glow... It sucked energy right out of Thadd's sword.

Brodin sucked in a breath and watched the gold energy flow into her glove.

Then she sent a blast toward the captain.

It hit Thadd mid chest and he flew backward, landing on his back.

Annora raced to him, and thankfully, Thadd seemed unharmed. He sat up, shaking his head.

He rose, his fierce scowl directed at Candela.

Rage flared in Annora's face.

Brodin attacked. He rammed into Candela's shield, and it knocked him back.

"Naveri," Annora cried. She ran and leaped into the air. Thadd lifted his hands, and a pulse of power lifted Annora higher.

She sailed straight up, then straight over Candela's shield.

With a curse, the warlord dodged, but Annora's kick connected with Candela's head. The woman cried out, her shield winking out of existence.

Suddenly, lights on the machine under them winked off.

"No!" Candela screamed. "*No.*"

Poppy's head popped up from the opening. She was beaming.

Brodin smiled. *She'd done it.*

Candela made an infuriated sound. She scrambled to her feet and held up her palm. Energy gathered, pulled from all around them. She aimed it at Poppy.

No. Brodin was already moving, but he was too far away to stop it.

Annora leaped in between Poppy and the warlord.

The blast lifted her off her feet, and flung her off the edge of the machine.

Brodin's chest locked. She was tumbling over and over. She wouldn't land on her feet. She'd break every bone in her body.

Thadd cursed, shoved his sword in its scabbard, and ran. With a powerful leap, he sailed into the air.

With a pulse of energy, he sailed high, and caught Annora in his arms. The pair dropped out of sight.

Sucking his anger deeper, Brodin morphed, growing larger and more muscular in his semi-shift. His claws grew longer.

Poppy stepped up behind him.

He growled. "This is the end, Candela."

"IT WON'T END HERE," Candela drawled. "Your father is relentless. He'll never stop."

Poppy heard Brodin growl again, the terrifying sound raising the hairs on her arms.

She stepped closer to him; his muscular back was tense, and every muscle strained.

"For now, I'll take killing you and destroying your machine," Brodin said.

"It's filled with my sweet Damari poison. You might've set me back, but I don't give up, either."

"You can't hurt anyone if you're dead." Brodin charged, his claws out. Her shield went up.

He hit it and kept up the pressure.

Through the blue glimmer, he saw her grimace.

Brodin pushed, using all his strength and Candela slid backward. He kept pushing and she looked back over her shoulder. The edge was getting closer.

"Your soft Zhylaw bones won't survive a long fall, will they?" he said.

"You're just an animal relying on brute strength."

"Is that supposed to be an insult?" He shoved her harder.

Poppy moved closer, willing her own strength into Brodin. Just a little bit farther, and this would all be over.

Candela's face twisted. She glared at Poppy. "If not for you, he'd be drowning in guilt and rage, grieving for all his dead. I would've watched the dirty wolves descend into madness."

"You are the worst kind of evil," Poppy said. "Seeing others as beneath you. As things you can torture and hurt. I'll enjoy seeing the end of you."

Suddenly, Candela released her shield. Brodin lurched forward, but Candela dropped to the ground.

Then she leaped at Poppy, like a sprinter off the blocks.

Oh, God.

Poppy threw herself sideways. Candela's metal claws bit into Poppy's legs.

"I'll kill you. I'll kill him." She raised her claws and aimed at Poppy's face.

Poppy growled. She was no one's prey or victim.

She whipped her own claws up and slashed at Candela's face.

The warlord screamed and rolled away, her face bleeding.

Brodin slammed into her. He grabbed Candela's neck and lifted her off the ground.

She seemed strangely calm for someone staring at a terrifying, fierce, part-man, part-wolf.

Then Poppy saw Candela's hand slide into her pocket.

Poppy frowned. "Brodin, she's reaching for something!"

She lifted a vial of green fluid. She smashed it against Brodin's chest.

Poppy smelled the horrid scent. Brodin dropped Candela and staggered back, clawing at his throat.

His eyes were bleeding to black.

The Damari poison. *No.*

Candela laughed wildly. Poppy was so sick of this bitch laughing.

"It's a concentrated dose. Thirty times stronger." Candela's eyes met Poppy's. "Not even you will be able to calm him."

Poppy's gut curdled, her chest hitched.

No. No. No.

Brodin's muscles rolled under his skin, and he got even bigger. His claws grew impossibly long, and jagged fangs grew out of his mouth. The bones in his face changed to a nightmarish meld of wolf and man.

Every muscle strained, quivering.

He was fighting it. Or trying to.

He threw his head back and howled.

Anger punched through Poppy. Brodin fought hard for his people. He had built a world, a community, and ensured his people didn't surrender to their animal half. All Candela did was destroy.

With a howl of her own, Poppy jumped on the warlord and knocked her to the ground. She sank her claws into Candela's shoulder. The warlord fought and twisted, but Poppy used all her strength.

Then the nightmare version of Brodin dropped down beside them.

Poppy froze. He sniffed her, those black eyes showing no recognition.

He sniffed Candela and snarled.

Brodin was still in there, somewhere.

"Help me," Poppy said.

That black gaze met hers, then he pinned Candela's shoulders down.

"He'll kill you," Candela spat. "He'll lose control, then slice you open and eat your innards."

"Shut up." Poppy rammed her claws into Candela's chest.

The warlord jerked, but Brodin growled and held her.

Poppy twisted her claws.

Blood spilled from Candela's mouth. "You will...be dead too. He'll kill you."

"Just die, damn you." Poppy leaned all her weight forward.

A second later, Candela jerked and coughed. Then she went still, her single eye frozen open.

Panting, Poppy pulled her claws free.

God.

Hot breath brushed against the back of her neck, and she heard a low growl.

Everything inside her froze.

She slowly turned.

She was inches away from the nightmare monster with black eyes.

She couldn't see Brodin in them anywhere.

"Brodin, it's Poppy."

He growled again.

"Fight it, please." She tried to emanate calm, but it didn't seem to be having any effect on him. "You know me. Poppy. You're Brodin. The Emperor of Damar."

He cocked his head.

Suddenly, she rose, and he did, too. When she stepped back, he tensed.

Then his gaze tracked to the side. She followed, and saw Annora and Thadd crouched at the edge of the machine.

Annora's hair was loose, Thadd's chest was streaked with blood.

"She infected him," Poppy said.

Brodin snarled.

"Come this way slowly," Annora said.

Poppy shook her head. "We have to help him."

Brodin whirled and grabbed her. She let out a squeak, and he lifted her off her feet and yanked her up.

He growled in her face.

Fear threatened to take over her mind. "Brodin, please."

"Poppy, there are more Zhylaw cats on the way," Annora said. "They are starting to climb the machine."

"Go," Poppy said.

"No, we—"

"Go. I'll be fine." She didn't take her gaze off Brodin's.

She sensed Annora and Thadd move away.

"Come back to me, Brodin. I love you. It's crazy. I crashed on the other side of the galaxy and fell in love with an alien, shapeshifter king. The way you look at me... No one's looked at me like that before." Her voice cracked. "Please look at me like that again."

He glared at her. Then he set her down.

She pulled in a breath. "Brodin —"

His big body jerked, and he made an angry, pained sound. His veins bulged.

The black in his eyes was churning. His head bowed.

"Brodin," she whispered. She wanted to help him.

She reached for him, and his head whipped up, fierce. He moved—

And rammed his claws into her belly.

For a second, there was no pain, and she just stared at him in shock.

CHAPTER EIGHTEEN

He smelled fresh blood.

Wild, violent urges hammered through him.

The tiny prey in front of him blinked up at him. Some part of him, buried deep, tried to push free.

He growled. The blood smelled so good. He wanted to hunt, fight, and win.

"It's okay, Brodin." His prey pulled in a shaky breath. "I love you." She gave him a sad smile. "Even if I don't get...to be with you, I'll always love you." A trickle of blood came out of the corner of her mouth. "Don't blame yourself, my gorgeous wolf. Promise me that."

Her blue eyes—steady, shining with intelligence—stayed locked on his.

"I love you."

He cocked his head, couldn't look away. He felt a warmth growing in his chest, melting the ice. It swelled, and he growled.

Then it burst to life.

He knew what it was. The mating tie.

The connection between two mates.

He shuddered, and saw her jerk, her eyes going wide.

The violent, wild emotion storming inside him shrank away, and love washed through him. His head cleared.

"Brodin," she whispered.

"Poppy," he breathed. He could think again.

Then he looked down and stared at where his claws were buried in her stomach.

No. With horror, he yanked them free.

She collapsed and he caught her. He lowered her to the ground.

"Poppy. *Poppy*."

"It's...okay."

It wasn't. He could see the blood pooling under her. So much blood. Pain was clouding her eyes.

It wasn't okay. Not at all.

"I hurt you." The words ripped out of him.

She moved her hand, clumsily reaching for his.

He grabbed her fingers and held on tight.

"I love you, Brodin."

His chest swelled. *Gorr*. "Poppy, I love you, too. My entire life, I've been groomed to lead my people, to stand between them and Zavir."

"You're a wonderful king. Brave, smart, steadfast."

"But you love me. Brodin. A man who loses his temper."

She smiled at him. "Who likes to escape to his lair, and take a bath, and read a book."

He leaned down and kissed her. "And who loves a small, smart, brave, and sometimes foolish woman from

Earth." Emotion flooded him, his stomach tight. "Don't leave me, Poppy. I... I can't bear this."

"Brodin—"

She grimaced. She was in pain, and he pressed a hand on her belly, trying to stop the blood loss.

He cupped her cheek and saw her blood on his fingers. Poppy's blood.

Fear like he'd never known filled him. But he felt something else—the tie between them.

Poppy was his mate. He felt a connection. *Gorr*, she was weak and fading.

He poured his own strength into her.

Her eyes widened. "What are you doing?"

"You're my mate."

"Mate?"

"We're linked. Damari wolves mate for life. It means we generate pheromones that only affect our mate. Linking us. Always."

"Brodin—"

"You'll always want me, even when I'm old and gray and wrinkled."

"I can't imagine not wanting you." She shuddered, pulling in a breath. "What happens if a mate dies?"

His hands clenched on her. "Poppy, please..."

"Tell me."

"The remaining mate pines for the rest of their lives. A shadow of their former selves."

"You won't do that."

"I will."

"You'll live," she snapped.

"I need to live with you." He pressed his mouth to hers.

Brodin fought back his despair. He poured more of his life force into her, but she needed a healer. And she was too hurt to move.

He sensed movement to his right. Growling, he crouched over her protectively.

A man walked forward, relaxed and calm. He moved well—was fit and lean. He had a regal face, and didn't look young or old. His dark hair was well cut.

"What the *gorr* are you doing here?" Brodin demanded.

Brodin's father held out his hands. "I wanted to check on Candela. She has a habit of veering off plan."

"The plan being to annihilate my people."

Zavir sighed. "That wasn't the plan."

Brodin snarled. "You sent her."

Zavir's gaze shifted to Poppy. She was only semiconscious now.

"Because of Candela, my mate is dying." Brodin wanted to howl, scream.

His father knelt and Brodin tensed. Zavir held up his hands.

"I won't hurt her."

Brodin blew out a breath.

Zavir pulled out a device. It was a long, slim wand.

Brodin stiffened. "Can you help her?"

"Maybe."

"Do it, or I'll gut you."

The device glowed, and he held it over Poppy's stomach.

"She's not Damari," Zavir said, tone loaded with curiosity. "She's infected, but not full Damari."

If he didn't give the man any information, he'd just send people to find out himself. "She's from Earth. Krastin abducted her from the wreckage of a crash on Zhalto, and experimented on her. He used one of my abducted hunters." Brodin spat the words. "This is all your fault, as always, Zavir."

There was a glint of frustration in Zavir's eyes. "I wish you'd call me father." He focused back on Poppy.

Brodin wished Zavir looked more evil. The few times he'd met the man, he always looked and acted like someone you wanted to know.

"She's strong," Zavir said. "A good match. I approve."

"Like I care."

Zavir sighed. "There."

Poppy's eyes fluttered open. "Brodin?"

"Hey." He pulled her into his arms. He shuddered with relief.

"I'm all right." She hugged him back. "I think." She touched her stomach. "Oh, there's a lot of blood."

"Move slowly," Zavir said. "She'll need fluids."

Her gaze shifted to Zavir and she blinked. "Who are you?"

Zavir smiled. "Family."

Brodin growled and pulled her closer. "He is *not* family, and he's not welcome."

"I healed her."

"Thank you. Now leave Damar."

Zavir continued to smile at Poppy. "My son has never had polite manners. I'm Zavir."

Poppy made a strangled sound and pulled away from him.

Zavir didn't look offended. "She's loyal." His gaze moved back to Brodin. "I want you to join me, my son. We can do so much good for Damar, for Sarkan, for the entire system."

"No."

Shaking his head, Zavir stood. "So stubborn, like your mother." He glanced around. "I'm proud of you."

Gorr. Brodin didn't know how he could hate a man so much, while a part of him also liked him.

It was why Zavir was so dangerous.

"Stop interfering with our planets, Zavir. Leave us to rule ourselves."

A self-depreciating smile crossed the man's face and he shrugged. "I can't. Wildness and stubbornness is in your genetic makeup; the need to rule is in mine. Take care of your mate, my son."

Zavir turned and walked away. He touched something on his belt and winked out of existence.

Brodin pulled Poppy closer and held on tight.

Candela was dead and Poppy was alive. That was all that mattered.

POPPY LEANED INTO BRODIN. She felt weak and lightheaded.

She could hardly believe that *Zavir* had healed her. She'd been dying. She'd felt herself drifting away.

But now, she was okay.

Zavir hadn't looked like the evil, twisted monster she'd pictured in her head. She'd even seen emotion on the man's face when he looked at Brodin.

It might be twisted, but somewhere, deep inside, he cared about his son.

Brodin's arms tightened on her. That's when she felt the strong warmth inside her. She couldn't exactly describe it, but it felt like Brodin—strong, unyielding, steady as a rock.

"So we're mated," she said.

He lifted his head and looked down at her. "Yes. You're mine now, Poppy Ellison. You are right where you belong."

God. She'd never felt like she belonged anywhere or to anyone. Growing up, she'd tried not to let it bother her or slow her down, but now she felt like she'd found her place.

Millions of light-years from Earth. On an alien, shapeshifter planet, with a big, strong, alien emperor.

"I love you, Brodin. If I'm yours, that must mean that you're mine."

There was a low rumble in his chest. His lips touched hers. It always amazed her that this tough, immensely strong wolf could also be gentle.

"Yes, I give you my loyalty, my body, my love, my life."

Warmth filled her. "Brodin—"

"I'll protect you, support you, give you a home, and, one day, children."

Oh, God. Tears welled. She'd never imagined it was

possible to feel this much for one person. She pulled him closer. "You didn't let me go."

"I never will." He lifted her into his arms. "Now, how about we get out of here?"

She nodded.

Then the machine gave a low, resonant beep.

Poppy frowned. *Shit.* Was it somehow turning itself back on?

Nearby, one panel lit up.

Scowling, Brodin moved closer.

"Self-destruct sequence initiated," a computerized voice said. "Evacuate blast zone."

Poppy went rock solid. Brodin's arms convulsed on her.

"We need to go," he said urgently. "Now!"

He ran to the edge of the machine and jumped.

They sailed through the air, and her heart lodged in her throat. They landed on a lower ledge, then he jumped again.

She clung to him, knowing he'd keep her safe. She still felt weak, and her vision was blurry at the edges. Her brain felt sluggish, and she was barely holding on to consciousness.

Brodin landed on the ground. "Hold on, Poppy."

"I am."

"Brodin!" Thadd's deep voice echoed from nearby.

Poppy turned her head and saw the captain decapitate a Zhylaw cat with his sword—a stream of gold energy flowing off it.

Next to him, Annora rammed her claws into another

cat. She was moving awkwardly, one leg covered in blood.

"Are you okay?" his First Claw yelled.

Brodin nodded. "We have to go. The machine is set to self-destruct."

Both Thadd and Annora cursed.

"The young ones?" Brodin asked.

"The other cleavers got them out."

Thank God. Hopefully, they were all out of the lake and safe.

"We need to move fast." Thadd shoved his sword in its sheath. Then he swept Annora off her feet.

"Put me down, Naveri."

"No."

"I can walk."

"That cat clawed up your leg. You'll be too slow."

Her face twisted, then she ran her arm along his broad shoulders. "Fine."

"So glad you saw reason for a change, Rahl."

"Don't push it."

Poppy hid her smile.

Behind them, the machine started to glow a bright white.

"Move!" Brodin roared.

He sprinted out of the dome and into the corridor. Poppy clung to him. Thadd and Annora were right behind them. They raced fast, through the twists and turns of the ship, and reached the moon pool they'd used to enter. Brodin spun so Poppy was face-to-face with him, and she clamped herself to his chest.

"Don't let go," he told her.

"Never."

They stuck their re-breathers in place and then plunged into the water.

Poppy was too tired to swim. She simply held onto Brodin, and tried not to get in his way. He kicked powerfully through the water. She couldn't see Thadd and Annora, but she knew they must be close.

Her breathing echoed in her ears, and she decided that deep-water diving really wasn't her thing. The light grew brighter.

Finally, they broke the surface. She tore the device out of her mouth, and dragged in a breath of fresh air.

The shore wasn't far away, and she saw the cleavers there.

Thadd and Annora's heads appeared.

On the shore, the cleavers cheered.

Brodin held Poppy as he kicked toward the others. He carried her out of the lake, water streaming off them. Thadd did the same with Annora.

"Put me down now, Captain," Annora muttered.

"In a minute."

That elicited a low, feminine growl.

"Is everyone all right?" Brodin asked.

"The young ones are all alive, but Stein and Phelan are hurt," Tolf said. "They haven't regained consciousness."

Oh, no. Poppy's belly cramped.

Annora finally broke free of Thadd and hobbled across the rocky shore. "*Nayla.*"

A wet, bedraggled girl with dark eyes looked up.

She'd be pretty when she wasn't pale, soaked, scared, and exhausted.

"Nora." The girl launched herself at her sister.

The force of the hug almost caused Annora's injured leg to collapse, but moving lightning-fast, Thadd appeared behind Annora and held the pair up.

She flashed the captain a look, before she wrapped her arms more tightly around her sister.

"By the wolves," someone called out. "What's happening in the lake?"

Poppy swiveled in Brodin's arms.

The water in the center of the lake was bubbling.

"Back up," he ordered.

They did. Two cleavers lifted the unconscious teenagers and shifted them.

Then, there was a muted boom.

The water in the lake shot up into the sky in a huge plume. There were gasps and shouts.

Then, the water fell back down. The lake was choppy, and a wave washed up onto the shore, touching their feet.

"The machine's destroyed," she murmured.

"All thanks to you," Brodin said.

She smiled. "It was a team effort." Then she studied the water. "The poison could still be in there. I suggest you get your people to test the lake."

He nodded.

"Candela's dead?" A teenager with a pale, handsome, but very bruised face asked.

"She's dead," Brodin said. "My mate, our runa, killed her."

Cheers erupted.

Thadd and Annora hobbled over.

"You beat the poison," Annora said quietly.

"Barely." Brodin pulled Poppy close and she leaned into him. "Poppy helped me. The mating tie kicked in."

A faint smile crossed his First Claw's face. "I knew you two were mates."

"Under the influence of the poison, I hurt her." Brodin cupped Poppy's cheek.

"It wasn't your fault."

Thadd eyed her bloodstained shirt. "But you're healed?"

Brodin released a breath. "Zavir healed her."

Both Thadd and Annora sucked in sharp breaths.

"He was here?" Thadd spat the words.

Brodin nodded.

"He healed Poppy?" Annora asked, confused.

Brodin nodded again. "For me." His eyes were churning.

"Do you think he was still in the ship?" Thadd asked.

"No." Brodin looked up into the sky. "He got away."

Poppy held her mate tighter, and then her vision started to blur. *Oh, no.* She gripped him harder.

"Poppy?" His brow creased.

"I think I'm going to faint."

He cursed and lifted her.

"But don't worry, I'll be fine, my sexy mate," she whispered.

"You will be," he said. "I'll make sure of it."

CHAPTER NINETEEN

Brodin carried the large bunch of wildflowers up the stairs to his bedroom.

Light poured in the window, and his gaze went straight to the woman in his bed. His body filled with so many emotions he couldn't sort them all out.

He didn't want to.

Poppy gave him a disgruntled look. "I've been 'resting' for three days, and you've been hovering over me the entire time. I'm *fine*. I want out of this bed, Brodin."

He'd heard multiple variations of the speech over the last day. The side table beside the bed was filled with a multitude of small mechanica. He'd given her metal, parts, and tools to keep her busy while on bedrest, and she'd made some of the best mechanica he'd seen.

There was an entire pack of wolves, that walked and howled. Each one was detailed and different. She'd also made several interesting animals from Earth—a bear, a lion, a zebra, and some strange thing called a kangaroo. He was certain she'd made that one up.

He held out the flowers.

Her face softened. "They're beautiful, but don't distract me."

"I picked them myself from the forest."

"Damn, you're distracting me." She took the flowers and sniffed them. "They are beautiful, Brodin."

He sat on the bed beside her. "I know you're healed, but you lost a lot of blood."

He'd never forget the terror of holding her in his arms, knowing she was dying.

"Brodin." She set the flowers aside and slithered onto his lap. "I'm right here."

He knew that as his mate, she could sense his emotions. He wrapped his arms around her. He still hated Zavir, but his father had done one thing Brodin would always be grateful for.

Poppy nipped his jaw. "I'm not made of glass, Brodin Damar Sarkany."

"I know, my beautiful mate, but I want to spoil you, make sure you are better."

The look on her face filled his heart.

"No one's ever called me beautiful," she said.

"The men of Earth really are empty-headed fools. They never deserved you." He nuzzled her and drew in her scent. "And now you're mine."

Love shone in her eyes. "I never knew I could love someone as much as I love you."

With a growl, he kissed her.

She kissed him back, but then broke free before it got very far. "No. Don't get me all hot and bothered, and then don't follow through. Again." Her disgruntlement was plain to hear.

Cassanra had issued a no-exertion rule. Every time Poppy had instigated kissing and touching, Brodin had put a stop to it going any further.

His sexy mate had protested vocally.

Of course, she wasn't aware that Cassanra had given her a clean bill of health this morning.

"How are Thadd, Annora, and the kids?" Poppy asked.

Brodin dialed back his desire. He'd had a lot of practice over the last few frustrating days. "Thadd is fine. He's been checking in on Annora as her leg heals. Her leg's going to be fine."

Poppy blew out a breath. "Good."

"Annora threw a jug at Thadd's head this morning. Luckily the Zhalton has fast reflexes."

Poppy's lips twitched. "They do seem to strike sparks off each other."

Brodin grunted. "More like a forest fire." He toyed with her silky hair. "The teenagers are healing. Stein and Phelan will take a little longer, but the others, including Annora's sister, have been released."

"That's good to hear."

"Mal and Rhain arrive tomorrow."

A huge smile lit Poppy's face. "I can't wait to see Mal."

He felt the love and excitement throb off her, and his gut hardened. He caught her chin. "You're mine, Poppy."

"I know."

"You aren't going to live on Zhalto."

Her eyes flashed. "You haven't asked me to stay."

"You're my mate," he growled.

She bopped his nose with a finger. "I know, but a little romance wouldn't go astray."

He rolled, pinning her to the bed beneath him. He loved seeing the color, health, and strength back in her face.

"I brought you flowers. That's romance."

Her face softened. "And they are pretty."

"Poppy Ellison, would you be my mate and partner? Will you stay here on my world of Damar and make a home with me?"

"Brodin," she breathed, her eyes brimming.

"You and me, mates, together for a lifetime. Right here, I promise you that you will always belong here, with me. You were the missing piece I never knew I was looking for."

"Oh." Tears welled in her eyes.

"Don't cry."

"They're happy tears. And yes, Brodin, I want to stay here and belong with you, and make a home together."

He smiled, elation surging through him. "Good."

He kissed her.

She was dazed and breathless when he lifted his head. "I have something for you."

"Does it involve you getting naked?" she asked, in a disgruntled voice.

He smiled. "Patience." He pulled a small item from his pocket. "I spoke with Mal."

"Okay."

"She told me that on Earth, it's customary for mated

couples to wear a ring." He held up the ring he had commissioned for her.

She gasped, and her gaze flew to his face. "You told Mal we're mated?"

"Not yet. I was just asking general questions about Earth."

Poppy's gaze zeroed in on the ring. "Brodin, it's beautiful."

"It's perfect for you. It's a Damar Sapphire." It was the same color as her eyes.

It was a round hunk of stone—raw and wild like the Damari—set in silver metal mined from the south.

"Which finger?" he asked.

She held up her left hand and wiggled a finger. "This one."

He slid it on. It was a little loose, but he could have the jewel smith adjust it.

She held it up, pleasure on her face. "Can I get you a ring? Warn off any Damari females who get any ideas?"

"I'd be honored to wear anything you give me." He lowered his head and nibbled her bottom lip.

She pressed a hand to his shoulder. "Don't kiss me again. I can't handle being all turned on, and then having to stop."

He smiled. "Cassanra cleared you this morning."

Her lips parted. "Why didn't you say that earlier?" She shoved up, surprising him. She managed to roll him onto his back. Smiling, she straddled his hips.

She lowered her head, her mouth on his neck.

Brodin growled, desire filling his gut. His beautiful, sweet, sexy mate.

She bit his neck and he groaned, his fingers digging into her hips. He rolled her beneath him, and claimed her mouth with his.

The kiss was wild, filled with love and need, and the longing of mates.

Brodin ripped his clothes off, then tore at hers. When he saw the newly healed scars on her belly, he froze.

"Brodin," she said carefully.

He stroked them, sorry that Candela had poisoned him enough to make him do this.

Poppy slid a hand in his hair and tugged. "They're a sign we survived. That we won."

Gorr, she was amazing. Seeing the hope in the darkest of places.

He lowered his head and kissed each mark.

Then he moved lower.

Soon, she was writhing beneath him, her breathing coming in pants.

"Brodin... I need you."

He pushed her legs wide, then drove his cock inside her.

Poppy gasped, her fingers digging into his muscles.

"My sweet Poppy, my mate."

"I'm surrounded by you." She moaned. "Loved, protected, wanted, needed."

So much flared inside him. He withdrew, then surged back inside her. He drove into her—again and again. Soon, she was clawing at him. His thrusts became frenzied, and he rocked back on his knees, pulling her up. She cried out, his cock deep inside her. Then he tilted her head and bit her neck.

That set off her orgasm, and as she shuddered against him, it triggered his own. He pressed her forward, and came inside his mate.

POPPY PRACTICALLY SKIPPED down the path under the trees.

Some Damari kids ran past, a few in their tiny wolf form. She laughed and waved. They giggled and gave cute, little howls.

She had a flower from her bouquet tucked behind her ear. She breathed the scent of it in. She was in love. She was loved.

She stopped and looked at Accalia spread out before her. A part of her would miss Earth, and her parents.

But she belonged here now.

She'd embrace her life on Damar with her gorgeous mate. She lifted her hand and the jewel on her ring glinted in the sunlight.

Brodin loved her. They'd make a life together, and she'd help him rule Damar, and grow old at his side.

She could learn more about the technology here, and use her skills. The head of the science team had already reached out to her and asked her to look at the solar-power generators.

Yes, it felt very nice to belong.

She headed down the path leading toward the landing pads. Her pulse skipped with excitement.

Mal was on her way, for a visit with her overlord.

Poppy grinned. They were coming to collect Thadd, but also so Mal and Poppy could see each other.

She was so excited. She also knew that Graylan was coming from Taln. Tonight, they'd have a feast, and it was a chance for the brothers to discuss Zavir.

They'd beaten Candela, but no one believed that Zavir had given up.

She neared the cleaver lodge. Just beyond it sat a sleek, modern cabin built into the boulders nearby. She knew it was Annora's place.

Suddenly, the front door flung open, and Annora stalked out.

The First Claw wore fitted pants, and a red top. Her long hair was loose for a change. Wow, it was gorgeous. It also looked like her leg had healed well.

Thadd stormed out the door after her.

The pair spun to face each other, clearly arguing.

Hmm. Working together to fight Candela obviously hadn't smoothed the relationship between these two. They—

Annora grabbed the front of Thadd's shirt, yanked him closer, and kissed him.

Thadd shifted, cupped Annora's ass, and lifted her off her feet. She wrapped her long legs around his hips, and he backed her against the side of the house, and they went at it.

Oh. *Oh.* Poppy stared, her eyes wide.

Well, she wasn't sure what to do about *this* situation. If she moved, they might notice her. If...

Annora ripped her mouth free of Thadd's and looked over his broad shoulder. Her gaze collided with Poppy's.

Um. Poppy felt like a deer caught in a pair of headlights.

Annora struggled against Thadd until he put her down. He said something, Annora shook her head. Then she strode off, her long legs moving fast.

Thadd put his hands on his hips, looked at the sky, and very clearly muttered a curse. Then, he stalked off in the opposite direction.

Poppy cleared her throat and grinned. It would be fun to see where *that* ended up.

She followed the path the rest of the way to the hill where the landing pads were situated. She rode up in the elevator, and when she came out at the top, she spotted the big, hunky form of her mate. Her belly warmed.

Sensing her approach, Brodin turned and smiled.

She went straight to him, and he kissed her.

"Hello, my mate," Brodin drawled.

"Hi."

He rubbed his nose against hers. "I want to toss you over my shoulder and take you to the lair."

"Soon. I want to see Mal first."

"The shuttle just hit atmosphere."

Moments later, she spotted the silver Zhalton ship in the sky. Thadd arrived, as did Annora. The two studiously ignored each other.

The shuttle landed, and Poppy was bursting with excitement. Brodin squeezed her hand.

The doors opened.

Mal rushed out. She was a tall, athletic woman. Her brown braid whipped out behind her.

"Mal!" Poppy broke into a run.

"Poppy!"

Mal met her halfway. They collided and wrapped their arms around each other.

They were laughing, crying.

"God, I am so glad you're okay," Mal said. "You look great. Glowing."

"You, too."

"Well, it's probably thanks to my man, and all the energy I'm wielding these days."

Poppy looked at Rhain. The overlord was smiling at them.

He was just as tall, dark, and hot in real life.

"He's handsome," Poppy said.

"He's all mine." Mal nudged Poppy's hip. "I bet we can find you a hot, handsome Zhalton as well, Pop."

"Oh, well." Her cheeks flushed. She saw Brodin scowl and heard his sub-vocal growl.

"Brodin." Rhain turned to his brother. The men hugged, slapping each other's backs. "Well done on ousting Candela."

"Thanks for letting Thadd help. He was instrumental in tracking her down."

Thadd inclined his head.

"And thanks for taking good care of Poppy." Mal tossed an arm around Poppy's shoulders. "She looks great. Poppy, I can't wait for you to see Zhalto, and the capital city Citadel—"

"She's not going to Zhalto," Brodin said. "At least, not to live."

Mal frowned. "What do you mean?"

Poppy took Mal's hand and squeezed. "Mal, I'm going to make my home on Damar."

Mal blinked. "What?"

"With my mate."

Mal's eyes went wide. "Your mate?"

Poppy nodded.

Mal grinned. "You went and fell for a wolf?"

"It wasn't exactly a conscious choice," Poppy said. "It just happened."

"I know all about that. Well, is he sweet, and nice, and—?"

Brodin stepped closer, and pulled Poppy back against his chest.

Mal went still.

Rhain started laughing.

"You were supposed to heal her, not mate with her," Mal said.

"Like Poppy said, it wasn't a choice." He cupped Poppy's cheek. "I was helpless against my sweet mate from Earth. And now I'm helplessly in love."

"*Brodin,*" Poppy said.

He kissed her, and soon, she heard Mal's delighted laugh join Rhain's.

Then after that, all Poppy could think of was her mate.

CHAPTER TWENTY

Leaning back in his chair, Brodin enjoyed the talk and laughter around the table.

A long table had been set up in the dining room—with all his cleavers, the healers, Mal, Rhain, and Thadd, and Graylan sitting at it.

Graylan sat to Brodin's left.

Poppy was to his right. Then Rhain and Mal.

Mal and Poppy were laughing over some story involving an unpleasant woman called Dr. Wheeler. He watched the women, who were laughing so hard they had tears in their eyes.

They were so resilient. After everything they'd been through, they were making the most of every little thing.

They could never return to Earth, but they weren't letting that fact sadden them. He caught Rhain's gaze. His brother was watching the women, too.

They shared a smile.

Brodin's gaze shifted, and landed on Annora. She wasn't smiling and was very carefully *not* looking at

Thadd when the captain looked her way. When he wasn't watching her, she shot him some unhappy glares.

"I'm very glad you stopped Candela and her plans, Brodin," Graylan said.

Gray radiated dark intensity. He had a long face with sharp cheekbones, and his black hair was cut short. His eyes gleamed gold, like polished coins.

Brodin sipped his brewed marpa beer. "Agreed. Without Poppy, we could've had a massacre."

"So, she's a runa," Rhain said.

"Yes. The first in centuries."

"These women from Earth are full of surprises." Graylan sipped his own drink, his gold eyes glowing. "You've both claimed the only ones nearby. I feel deprived."

"You ready to settle down, Gray?" Brodin asked.

"Oh, no. I like my privacy too much." Graylan smiled. "And variety when I require it."

"Gray," Rhain said. "Zavir will likely target you next."

Their brother nodded and leaned forward. "I've run extra patrols of my fighters, and have surveillance drones in the air. There's no sign of any incursions on Taln."

"Maybe he's given up?" Rhain suggested.

"No." Brodin scowled. "I saw him. Here on Damar."

"What?" Rhain said.

"Poppy was hurt. She was dying." His hand curled around his glass. "Zavir healed her. He said he can't give up, that it's not in his nature."

All three of them went quiet.

"He's planning a new strategy," Brodin said. "Direct

attacks by warlords haven't worked, so I suspect he'll try something else."

"He's tricky, cunning, and slippery," Rhain said.

"We'll be ready," Graylan said.

"Hey." Poppy put her hand over Brodin's.

Instantly, he felt a sense of calm. He smiled at her, and let out a breath.

"Enough about Zavir," she said.

"Hell, yeah," Mal agreed. "That man has sucked up enough of our time and energy for now. When, and if, he strikes again, we'll be ready. He doesn't understand the bond you three have."

Brodin watched Rhain kiss his woman's temple.

His gaze shifted to Poppy. She was smiling at Thadd.

Zavir didn't understand love. The love of brothers. Love of friends, the people you served and protected, or the woman you loved.

Brodin let himself relax and enjoy. He listened to Poppy pepper Graylan with questions about Taln and his abilities.

And then he enjoyed watching Mal and Poppy trying all the new foods on offer.

A while later, he noticed one of Gray's tall, lean fighters step up beside him and murmur something in his brother's ear.

Graylan stiffened, and caught Brodin's gaze, then Rhain's.

"Do you have some where we can talk?" he asked, quietly.

Brodin's gut hardened. He nodded and rose, catching

Annora's attention and jerking his head. Thadd and Rhain pushed back their chairs.

Noting that something was up, Poppy stood, concern on her face.

"Poppy," Brodin said. "Why don't you—?"

"Not worry my pretty little head?" she asked, tartly.

Mal raised a brow. "Maybe we should pick some flowers or bake something while you take care of important things."

Rhain looked like he was hiding a smile, and doing a terrible job of it.

Brodin cleared his throat. "I was going to suggest you join us."

Poppy stepped closer and kissed the underside of his jaw. "Of course, you were."

They filed into the cleaver meeting room, sitting around the long, wooden table.

Graylan remained standing. "We have probes throughout the system."

After Sarkan, Taln had the largest fleet of starships and space technology.

"Zavir was spotted on Andret," Gray said.

Brodin steepled his hands. "Why would Zavir go to Andret?"

Poppy frowned. "Isn't it uninhabited?"

"It has no advanced life," Brodin said.

"But it is home to an unfriendly animal species," Rhain said. "Tentacle creatures called randis. They bore tunnels in the rock and feed on bacteria that grows in the magma under the crust. They're also attracted by vibrations and noise, and attack anything that lands on Andret."

Mal tapped her fingers on the table. "So why is Zavir there?"

Graylan pressed his hands to the table. "Andret is mineral rich."

Brodin frowned. The planet did have lots of minerals, although the randis made it uneconomical to mine there.

"It appears that Zavir is mining genite," Gray said.

Rhain and Brodin stiffened.

"I knew he'd try something new," Brodin growled.

"What?" Poppy asked. "What's genite?"

"A mineral," Gray told her. "It's detrimental to Talnians."

"Detrimental?" Mal prompted.

"Prolonged exposure weakens us, and blocks our abilities," Graylan told her.

"He's planning to target Taln, and genite is a part of his plan," Poppy breathed.

Graylan gave a sharp nod, his eyes boiling. "It will put our most powerful warriors out of action."

"We need to send a covert team to Andret," Rhain said. "Stop Zavir mining the genite."

"And no Talnian can go," Brodin said. "Annora, are you up for a trip?"

His First Claw nodded. "Yes, Emperor."

"And I'll send Thadd and a team," Rhain said. "You can both jointly run the mission. Select your team members."

Annora's face went blank, she hesitated, but nodded.

A muscle ticked in Thadd's jaw. "Of course, Overlord."

"Go," Brodin ordered.

"I'll provide the ship and tech," Graylan said. "Zavir must be stopped."

WITH AN ARM THROUGH MAL'S, Poppy watched several Damari pick up instruments at the far end of the lodge hall.

The music started. It was wild, passionate, with a heavy beat. Some of the cleavers got up and started dancing. There was a lot of stomping and clapping. The music got faster, and the dancers whirled—Damari balance, grace, and agility were on display. It reminded Poppy of Cossack dancing.

"Wow!" Mal clapped. "I like this."

Of course, Mal would. She'd always been a little wilder, and lived life her own way.

"Happy?" Poppy asked.

Mal met her gaze. "Yes. I sometimes feel like I should feel sad that I can't go back to Earth." Her gaze tracked to Rhain. A faint smile crossed her lips. "But I'm not. What I feel for Rhain... It's huge, scary-huge, but so damn good. I'm happier than I've ever been."

"Even knowing you'll be queen of an entire planet?" Poppy bumped her friend's shoulder playfully.

"Okay, that still freaks me out, a lot, but Rhain will help me." She pulled a face. "As will super bossy Thadd and his even bossier mother. Rhain's mom was killed years ago, so Thadd's mom is like a second mother to him. I'm going to have an intimidating countess for a mother-in-law."

"By the way, speaking of Thadd..."

Mal's gaze narrowed. "What? I know he still hasn't recovered after being tortured by Krastin."

"I saw him and Annora going at it."

"Those two are like jet fuel and flames. They're always fighting."

"Not going at it like that. I mean kissing. Hot, heavy, angry kissing."

"No way!"

A few heads swiveled in their direction.

"Way," Poppy said quietly.

"And now they're on a mission together." Mal tapped a finger against her chin. "Hmm. I think the attractive First Claw might be just what Captain Naveri needs right now." Mal grinned. "Oh, I love this." She looked back at Poppy. "I didn't ask if you are happy?"

"Can't you tell?"

"Well, every time you look at the rugged gorgeousness of Brodin, you get this look on your face."

"He loves me."

"You're lovable. I've always hated that you've never believed that."

"I love him, and we fit."

Mal smiled. "I get it. Totally. I'm sorry about your work and your parents."

Poppy nodded. "I can find work here. I miss my parents more than I thought."

"Your parents know you're alive, so that must be a

comfort for them. Sam Santos said if we ever visit Carthago, they can arrange a call back to Earth."

Poppy would look forward to that. She searched for Brodin and found him standing with his brothers. He noticed her looking and smiled. She smiled back.

"Oh, you guys are so cute," Mal said.

Poppy rolled her eyes. "So, when's your wedding?"

Her friend groaned. "I'm trying to convince Rhain to elope."

"I don't think the overlord of a planet can elope."

She groaned again. "The damn wedding gets bigger every time I look. The countess has me taking etiquette lessons." Mal grimaced.

Mal wouldn't love being on display, but she'd do fine.

"What about you and Brodin?" Mal asked.

"So, tradition is for Damari mates, and their closest friends and family, to have a private night ceremony under the full moon." Poppy thought it sounded magical.

"What? You don't have to have a huge wedding, with thousands watching, and a giant dress?"

Poppy smiled. "Apparently it's common for everyone at the ceremony to be barefoot."

"That's it. I'll trade you Rhain for Brodin."

"Excuse me?" a deep voice said.

Rhain, Brodin, and Graylan appeared.

"Oops." Mal smacked a kiss to Rhain's cheek. "Just joking, your Overlordness. But I like the small Damari wedding ceremony in the moonlight idea."

"I'm certain that if my warrior from Earth can take down a Zhylaw warlord and a pack of hexids, she can survive a wedding."

"Hmm." Mal nabbed his drink and sipped.

Brodin slid an arm around Poppy. She leaned against his hard chest.

"I am sorry we don't have an Earth woman for Graylan," Poppy said.

The man lifted his drink. "I'll just have to enjoy watching you two drive my brothers crazy."

Mal slapped Gray's arm.

"I'd like everyone's attention," Brodin said loudly, his voice echoing through the hall.

The room quieted.

"When my brother and his future queen asked for my help for her injured friend, I had no idea my world would change." His gaze dropped to Poppy's.

Her heart started beating hard in her chest.

"Poppy, from the moment I first saw you, your quiet strength, your courage, and your intelligence captured me. Later, your temper and...other assets held it."

There was a smattering of laughter.

"I am proud to call you my mate, my runa."

She melted against him.

"And to have you as my empress."

Empress? She went still. He hadn't mentioned that previously. *Yikes*.

Mal chuckled. "Empress Poppy. I love it."

Brodin tipped Poppy's chin up. "I love you. My life is forever yours."

"I love you too, Brodin. I'll stand by your side and stay there, for whatever challenges and triumphs we face together."

"To Brodin and Poppy," Rhain called out.

"Brodin and Poppy!"

He drew her close for a kiss. As the dancing resumed and conversation picked up, Brodin took her hand and led her into the moonlight.

"Where are you taking me?" she asked.

Suddenly, he dipped, then tossed her over his shoulder.

"Brodin!"

"I'm kidnapping my bride-to-be to have my way with her."

"Our guests—"

"We'll see them for breakfast." He jogged away into the forest. "We'll go to the lair, my sweet anata. Just you and me."

She smiled into the darkness. "Just you and me."

Poppy and Brodin. Her gorgeous alien mate.

As Brodin let out a long, deep howl that echoed through the forest, Poppy smiled. There was nowhere else she'd rather be.

I hope you enjoyed Poppy and Brodins's story!

GALACTIC KINGS continues with **CAPTAIN OF THE GUARD** starring Captain Thadd Naveri and First Claw Annora Rahl coming in May 2022.

If you'd like to know more about the Fortuna Station survivors on the desert planet of Carthago, then check out my action-packed science-fiction romance series,

Galactic Gladiators. **Read on for a preview of *Gladiator*, the first book in Galactic Gladiators, starring Harper and Raiden.**

Don't miss out! For updates about new releases, action romance info, free books, and other fun stuff, sign up for my VIP mailing list and get your *free box set* containing three action-packed romances.

Visit here to get started: www.annahackett.com

Would you like a FREE BOX SET of my books?

PREVIEW: GLADIATOR

Just another day at the office.

Harper Adams pulled herself along the outside of the space station module. She could hear her quiet breathing inside her spacesuit, and she easily pulled her weightless body along the slick, white surface of the module. She stopped to check a security panel, ensuring all the systems were running smoothly.

Check. Same as it had been yesterday, and the day

before that. But Harper never ever let herself forget that they were six hundred million kilometers away from Earth. That meant they were dependent only on themselves. She tapped some buttons on the security panel before closing the reinforced plastic cover. She liked to dot all her *I*s and cross all her *T*s. She never left anything to chance.

She grabbed the handholds and started pulling herself up over the cylindrical pod to check the panels on the other side. Glancing back behind herself, she caught a beautiful view of the planet below.

Harper stopped and made herself take it all in. The orange, white, and cream bands of Jupiter could take your breath away. Today, she could even see the famous superstorm of the Great Red Spot. She'd been on the Fortuna Research Station for almost eighteen months. That meant, despite the amazing view, she really didn't see it anymore.

She turned her head and looked down the length of the space station. At the end was the giant circular donut that housed the main living quarters and offices. The main ring rotated to provide artificial gravity for the residents. Lying off the center of the ring was the long cylinder of the research facility, and off that cylinder were several modules that housed various scientific labs and storage. At the far end of the station was the docking area for the supply ships that came from Earth every few months.

"Lieutenant Adams? Have you finished those checks?"

Harper heard the calm voice of her fellow space

marine and boss, Captain Samantha Santos, through the comm system in her helmet.

"Almost done," Harper answered.

"Take a good look at the botany module. The computer's showing some strange energy spikes, but the scientists in there said everything looks fine. Must be a system malfunction."

Which meant the geek squad engineers were going to have to come in and do some maintenance. "On it."

Harper swung her body around, and went feet-first down the other side of the module. She knew the rest of the security team—all made up of United Nations Space Marines—would be running similar checks on the other modules across the station. They had a great team to ensure the safety of the hundreds of scientists aboard the station. There was also a dedicated team of engineers that kept the guts of the station running.

She passed a large, solid window into the module, and could see various scientists floating around benches filled with all kinds of plants. They all wore matching gray jumpsuits accented with bright-blue at the collars, that indicated science team. There was a vast mix of scientists and disciplines aboard—biologists, botanists, chemists, astronomers, physicists, medical experts, and the list went on. All of them were conducting experiments, and some were searching for alien life beyond the edge of the solar system. It seemed like every other week, more probes were being sent out to hunt for radio signals or collect samples.

Since humans had perfected large solar sails as a way to safely and quickly propel spacecraft, getting around the solar system had become a lot easier. With radiation pressure exerted by sunlight onto the mirrored sails, they could travel from Earth to Fortuna Station orbiting Jupiter in just a few months. And many of the scientists aboard the station were looking beyond the solar system, planning manned expeditions farther and farther away. Harper wasn't sure they were quite ready for that.

She quickly checked the adjacent control panel. Among all the green lights, she spotted one that was blinking red, and she frowned. They definitely had a problem with the locking system on the exterior door at the end of the module. She activated the small propulsion pack on her spacesuit, and circled around the module. She slowed down as she passed the large, round exterior door at the end of the cylindrical module.

It was all locked into place and looked secure.

As she moved back to the module, she grabbed a handhold and then tapped the small tablet attached to the forearm of her suit. She keyed in a request for maintenance to come and check it.

She looked up and realized she was right near another window. Through the reinforced glass, a pretty, curvy blonde woman looked up and spotted Harper. She smiled and waved. Harper couldn't help but smile and lifted her gloved hand in greeting.

Dr. Regan Forrest was a botanist and a few years younger than Harper. The young woman was so open and friendly, and had befriended Harper from her first day on the station. Harper had never had a lot of friends —mainly because she'd been too busy raising her younger sister and working. She'd never had time for girly nights out or gossip.

But Regan was friendly, smart, and had the heart of a steamroller under her pretty exterior. Harper always had trouble saying no to her. Maybe the woman reminded her a little of Brianna. At the thought of her sister, something twisted painfully in Harper's chest.

Regan floated over to the window and held up a small tablet. She'd typed in some words.

Cards tonight?

Harper had been teaching Regan how to play poker. The woman was terrible at it, and Harper beat her all the time. But Regan never gave up.

Harper nodded and held up two fingers to indicate a couple of hours. She was off-shift shortly, and then she had a sparring match with Regan's cousin, Rory—one of the station engineers—in the gym. Aurora "Call me Rory or I'll hit you" Fraser had been trained in mixed martial arts, and Harper found the female engineer a hell of a sparring partner. Rory was teaching Harper some martial arts moves and Harper was showing the woman some basic sword moves. Since she was little, Harper had been a keen fencer.

Regan grinned back and nodded. Then the woman's wide smile disappeared. She spun around, and through the glass Harper could see the other scientists all looking around, concerned. One scientist was spinning around, green plants floating in the air around him, along with fat droplets of water and some other green fluid. He'd clearly screwed up and let his experiment get free.

"Lieutenant Adams?" The captain's voice came through her helmet again. "Harper?"

There was a sense of urgency that made Harper's belly tighten. "Go ahead, Captain."

"We have an alarm sounding in the botany module. The computer says there is a risk of decompression."

Dammit. "I just checked the security panels. The locking mechanism on the exterior door is showing red. I did a visual inspection and it's closed up tight."

"Okay, we talked with the scientist in charge. Looks like one of her team let something loose in there. It isn't dangerous, but it must be messing with the alarm sensors. System's locked them all in there." She made an annoyed sound. "Idiots will have to stay there until engineering can get down there and free them."

Harper studied the room through the glass again. Some of the green liquid had floated over to another bench that contained various frothing cylinders on it. A second later, the cylinders shattered, their contents bubbling upward.

The scientists all moved to the back exit of the module, banging on the locked door. *Damn.* They were trapped.

Harper met Regan's gaze. Her friend's face was pale, and wisps of her blonde hair had escaped her ponytail, floating around her face.

"Captain," Harper said. "Something's wrong. The experiments have overflowed their containment." She could see the scientists were all coughing.

"Engineering is on the way," the captain said.

Harper pushed herself off, flying over the surface of

the module. She reached the control panel and saw that several other lights had turned red. They needed to get this under control and they needed to do it now.

"Harper!" The captain's panicked voice. "Decompression in progress!"

What the hell? The module jerked beneath Harper. She looked up and saw the exterior door blow off, flying away from the station.

Her heart stopped. That meant all the scientists were exposed to the vacuum of space.

Fuck. Harper pushed off again, sending herself flying toward the end of the module. She put her arms by her sides to help increase her speed. Through the window, she saw that most of the scientists had grabbed on to whatever they could hold on to. A few were pulling emergency breathers over their heads.

She reached the end of the pod and saw the damage. There was torn metal where the door had been ripped off. Inside the door, she knew there would be a temporary repair kit containing a sheet of high-tech nano fabric that could be stretched across the opening to reestablish pressure. But it needed to be put in place manually. Harper reached for the latch to release the repair kit.

Suddenly, a slim body shot out of the pod, her arms and legs kicking. Her mouth was wide open in a silent scream.

Regan. Harper didn't let herself think. She turned, pushed off and fired her propulsion system, arrowing after her friend.

"Security Team to the botany module," she yelled through her comm system. "Security Team to botany module. We have decompression. One scientist has been expelled. I'm going after her. I need someone that can help calm the others and get the module sealed again."

"Acknowledged, Lieutenant," Captain Santos answered. "I'm on my way."

Harper focused on reaching Regan. She was gaining on her. She saw that the woman had lost consciousness. She also knew that Regan had only a couple of minutes to survive out here. Harper let her training take over. She tapped the propulsion system controls, trying for more speed, as she maneuvered her way toward Regan.

As she got close, Harper reached out and wrapped her arm around the scientist. "I've got you."

Harper turned, at the same time clipping a safety line to the loops on Regan's jumpsuit. Then, she touched the controls and propelled them straight back towards the module. She kept her friend pulled tightly toward her chest. *Hold on, Regan.*

She was so still. It reminded Harper of holding Brianna's dead body in her arms. Harper's jaw tightened. She wouldn't let Regan die out here. The woman had dreamed of working in space, and worked her entire career to get here, even defying her family. Harper wasn't going to fail her.

As the module got closer, she saw that the security team had arrived. She saw the captain's long, muscled body as she and another man put up the nano fabric.

"Incoming. Keep the door open."

"Can't keep it open much longer, Adams," the captain replied. "Make it snappy."

Harper adjusted her course, and, a second later, she

shot through the door with Regan in her arms. Behind her, the captain and another huge security marine, Lieutenant Blaine Strong, pulled the stretchy fabric across the opening.

"Decompression contained," the computer intoned.

Harper released a breath. On the panel beside the door, she saw the lights turning green. The nano fabric wouldn't hold forever, but it would do until they got everyone out of here, and then got a maintenance team in here to fix the door.

"Oxygen levels at required levels," the computer said again.

"Good work, Lieutenant." Captain Sam Santos floated over. She was a tall woman with a strong face and brown hair she kept pulled back in a tight ponytail. She had curves she kept ruthlessly toned, and golden skin she always said was thanks to her Puerto Rican heritage.

"Thanks, Captain." Harper ripped her helmet off and looked down at Regan.

Her blonde hair was a wild tangle, her face was pale and marked by what everyone who worked in space called space hickeys—bruises caused by the skin's small blood vessels bursting when exposed to the vacuum of space. *Please be okay.*

"Here." Blaine appeared, holding a portable breather. The big man was an excellent marine. He was about six foot five with broad shoulders that stretched his spacesuit to the limit. She knew he was a few inches over the height limit for space operations, but he was a damn good marine, which must have gone in his favor. He had dark skin thanks to his African-American father and his handsome face made him popular with the station's single ladies, but mostly he worked and hung out with the other marines.

"Thanks." Harper slipped the clear mask over Regan's mouth.

"Nice work out there." Blaine patted her shoulder. "She's alive because of you."

Suddenly, Regan jerked, pulling in a hard breath.

"You're okay." Harper gripped Regan's shoulder. "Take it easy."

Regan looked around the module, dazed and panicky. Harper watched as Regan caught sight of the fabric stretched across the end of the module, and all the plants floating around inside.

"God," Regan said with a raspy gasp, her breath fogging up the dome of the breather. She shook her head, her gaze moving to Harper. "Thanks, Harper."

"Any time." Harper squeezed her friend's shoulder. "It's what I'm here for."

Regan managed a wan smile. "No, it's just you. You didn't have to fly out into space to rescue me. I'm grateful."

"Come on. We need to get you to the infirmary so they can check you out. Maybe put some cream on your hickeys."

"Hickeys?" Regan touched her face and groaned. "Oh, no. I'm going to get a ribbing."

"And you didn't even get them the pleasurable way."

A faint blush touched Regan's cheeks. "That's right. If I had, at least the ribbing would have been worth it."

With a relieved laugh, Harper looked over at her captain. "I'm going to get Regan to the infirmary."

The other woman nodded. "Good. We'll meet you back at the Security Center."

With a nod, Harper pushed off, keeping one arm around Regan, and they floated into the main part of the science facility. Soon, they moved through the entrance into the central hub of the space station. As the artificial gravity hit, Harper's boots thudded onto the floor. Beside her, Regan almost collapsed.

Harper took most of the woman's weight and helped her down the corridor. They pushed into the infirmary.

A gray-haired, barrel-chested man rushed over. "Decided to take an unscheduled spacewalk, Dr. Forrest?"

Regan smiled weakly. "Yes. Without a spacesuit."

The doctor made a tsking sound and then took her from Harper. "We'll get her all patched up."

Harper nodded. "I'll come and check on you later."

Regan grabbed her hand. "We have a blackjack game scheduled. I'm planning to win back all those chocolates you won off me."

Harper snorted. "You can try." It was good to see some life back in Regan's blue eyes.

As Harper strode out into the corridor, she ran a hand through her dark hair, tension slowly melting out of her shoulders. She really needed a beer. She tilted her neck one way and then the other, hearing the bones pop.

Just another day at the office. The image of Regan drifting away from the space station burst in her head.

Harper released a breath. She was okay. Regan was safe and alive. That was all that mattered.

With a shake of her head, Harper headed toward the Security Center. She needed to debrief with the captain and clock off. Then she could get out of her spacesuit and take the one-minute shower that they were all allotted.

That was the one thing she missed about Earth. Long, hot showers.

And swimming. She'd been a swimmer all her life and there were days she missed slicing through the water.

She walked along a long corridor, meeting a few people—mainly scientists. She reached a spot where there was a long bank of windows that afforded a lovely view of Jupiter, and space beyond it.

Stingy showers and unscheduled spacewalks aside, Harper had zero regrets about coming out into space. There'd been nothing left for her on Earth, and to her surprise, she'd made friends here on Fortuna.

As she stared out into the black, mesmerized by the twinkle of stars, she caught a small flash of light in the distance. She paused, frowning. What the hell was that?

She stared hard at the spot where she'd seen the flash. Nothing there but the pretty sprinkle of stars. Harper shook her head. Fatigue was playing tricks on her. It had to have just been a weird trick of the lights reflecting off the glass.

Pushing the strange sighting away, she continued on to the Security Center.

Galactic Gladiators

Gladiator

Warrior
Hero
Protector
Champion
Barbarian
Beast
Rogue
Guardian
Cyborg
Imperator
Hunter
Also Available as Audiobooks!

PREVIEW: EON WARRIORS AND HELL SQUAD

Looking for more action-packed science fiction romance? Check out *Eon Warriors,* starting with the first book in the series is *Edge of Eon.*

Framed for a crime she didn't commit, a wrongly-imprisoned space captain's only chance at freedom is to abduct a fearsome alien war commander.

Sub-Captain Eve Traynor knows a suicide mission when she sees one. With deadly insectoid aliens threatening to invade Earth, the planet's only chance of survival is to get the attention of the fierce Eon Warriors. But the Eon want nothing to do with Earth, and Eve wants nothing to do with abducting War Commander Davion Thann-Eon off his warship. But when Earth's Space Corps threaten her sisters, Eve will do anything to keep them safe, even if it means she might not make it back.

War Commander Davion Thann-Eon is taking his first vacation in years. Dedicated to keeping the Eon Empire safe, he's been born and bred to protect. But when he's attacked and snatched off his very own warship, he is shocked to find himself face-to-face with a bold, tough little Terran warrior. One who both infuriates and intrigues him.

When their shuttle is attacked by the ravenous insectoid Kantos, Eve and Davion crash land on the terrifying hunter planet known as Hunter7. A planet designed to test a warrior to his limits. Now, the pair must work together to survive, caught between the planet and its dangers, the Kantos hunting them down, and their own incendiary attraction.

Eon Warriors

Edge of Eon

Touch of Eon

Heart of Eon

Kiss of Eon

Mark of Eon

Claim of Eon

Storm of Eon

Soul of Eon
King of Eon
Also Available as Audiobooks!

Want to learn more about *Hell Squad*? Check out the first action-packed book in the series, *Marcus*.

In the aftermath of a deadly alien invasion, a band of survivors fights on...

In a world gone to hell, Elle Milton—once the darling of the Sydney social scene—has carved a role for herself as the communications officer for the toughest commando team fighting for humanity's survival—Hell Squad. It's her chance to make a difference and make up for horrible past mistakes...despite the fact that its battle-hardened commander never wanted her on his team.

When Hell Squad is tasked with destroying a strategic alien facility, Elle knows they need her skills in the field. But first she must go head to head with Marcus Steele and convince him she won't be a liability.

Marcus Steele is a warrior through and through. He fights to protect the innocent and give the human race a chance to survive. And that includes the beautiful, gutsy Elle who twists him up inside with a single look. The last thing he wants is to take her into a warzone, but soon they are thrown together battling both the alien invaders and their overwhelming attraction. And Marcus will learn just how much he'll sacrifice to keep her safe.

Hell Squad

Marcus

Cruz

Gabe

Reed

Roth

Noah

Shaw

Holmes

Niko

Finn

Devlin

Theron

Hemi

Ash

Levi

Manu

Griff

Dom

Survivors

Tane

Also Available as Audiobooks!

ALSO BY ANNA HACKETT

Norcross Security

The Investigator

The Troubleshooter

The Specialist

The Bodyguard

The Hacker

The Powerbroker

Billionaire Heists

Stealing from Mr. Rich

Blackmailing Mr. Bossman

Hacking Mr. CEO

Team 52

Mission: Her Protection

Mission: Her Rescue

Mission: Her Security

Mission: Her Defense

Mission: Her Safety

Mission: Her Freedom

Mission: Her Shield

Mission: Her Justice

Also Available as Audiobooks!

Treasure Hunter Security

Undiscovered

Uncharted

Unexplored

Unfathomed

Untraveled

Unmapped

Unidentified

Undetected

Also Available as Audiobooks!

Galactic Kings

Overlord

Eon Warriors

Edge of Eon

Touch of Eon

Heart of Eon

Kiss of Eon

Mark of Eon

Claim of Eon

Storm of Eon

Soul of Eon

King of Eon

Also Available as Audiobooks!

Galactic Gladiators: House of Rone

Sentinel

Defender

Centurion

Paladin

Guard

Weapons Master

Also Available as Audiobooks!

Galactic Gladiators

Gladiator

Warrior

Hero

Protector

Champion

Barbarian

Beast

Rogue

Guardian

Cyborg

Imperator

Hunter

Also Available as Audiobooks!

Hell Squad

Marcus

Cruz

Gabe

Reed

Roth

Noah

Shaw

Holmes

Niko

Finn

Devlin

Theron

Hemi

Ash

Levi

Manu

Griff

Dom

Survivors

Tane

Also Available as Audiobooks!

The Anomaly Series

Time Thief

Mind Raider

Soul Stealer

Salvation

Anomaly Series Box Set

The Phoenix Adventures

Among Galactic Ruins

At Star's End

In the Devil's Nebula

On a Rogue Planet

Beneath a Trojan Moon

Beyond Galaxy's Edge

On a Cyborg Planet

Return to Dark Earth

On a Barbarian World

Lost in Barbarian Space

Through Uncharted Space

Crashed on an Ice World

Perma Series

Winter Fusion

A Galactic Holiday

Warriors of the Wind

Tempest

Storm & Seduction

Fury & Darkness

Standalone Titles

Savage Dragon

Hunter's Surrender

One Night with the Wolf

For more information visit www.annahackett.com

ABOUT THE AUTHOR

I'm a USA Today bestselling romance author who's passionate about ***fast-paced, emotion-filled*** contemporary romantic suspense and science fiction romance. I love writing about people overcoming unbeatable odds and achieving seemingly impossible goals. I like to believe it's possible for all of us to do the same.

I live in Australia with my own personal hero and two very busy, always-on-the-move sons.

For release dates, behind-the-scenes info, free books, and other fun stuff, sign up for the latest news here:

Website: www.annahackett.com

Made in United States
Orlando, FL
22 June 2023